Don't think. Don't feel. Get out before everything crashes down around you.

He wanted to tell Sabrina everything—about the first time he'd held his baby daughter in his arms, about how trusting his little girl had been from the first time she squeezed his finger in her chubby little fist until the day he'd lost her.

"Sometimes, I just wish it would be over, even if I just find her—" He stopped, unable to say the word. "Gone. And then I feel selfish, like a man who doesn't deserve to get his daughter back."

"It's not selfish," she said, her voice fierce. "You don't deserve this."

She gripped him tighter, holding on as if she needed him as much as he'd let himself need her.

"Thank you," he whispered. "For everything."

She nodded, and he knew she understood. Feel too much, and he'd fall apart. "Anything you need, anytime, come find me," she said. "I'm here. No matter what, I'll always be here."

He covered one of her hands with his own and then took it away from his cheek. He couldn't bring himself to let it go right away, so he just nodded.

"Nothing lasts forever, Aaron. Not even this much grief."

TRACY MONTOYA

FINDING HIS CHILD

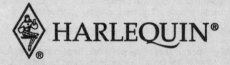

HARLEQUIN®

TORONTO • NEW YORK • LONDON
AMSTERDAM • PARIS • SYDNEY • HAMBURG
STOCKHOLM • ATHENS • TOKYO • MILAN • MADRID
PRAGUE • WARSAW • BUDAPEST • AUCKLAND

To Tom and Troy Rysavy, so you'll quit nagging me
about not dedicating—Ahem. To the coolest, sweetest,
best brothers ever. Love you guys!

ISBN-13: 978-0-373-88760-6
ISBN-10:   0-373-88760-4

FINDING HIS CHILD

Copyright © 2007 by Tracy Fernandez Rysavy

www.eHarlequin.com

Printed in U.S.A.

ABOUT THE AUTHOR

Tracy Montoya is a magazine editor for a crunchy nonprofit in Washington, D.C., though at present she's telecommuting from her house in Seoul, Korea. She lives with a psychotic cat, a lovable yet daft lhasa apso and a husband who's turned their home into the Island of Lost/Broken/Strange–Looking Antiques. A member of the National Association of Hispanic Journalists and the Society of Environmental Journalists, Tracy has written about everything, including Booker Prize–winning poet Martín Espada, socially responsible mutual funds to soap opera summits. Her articles have appeared in a variety of publications, such as *Hope, Utne Reader, Satya, YES!, Natural Home* and *New York Naturally*. Prior to launching her journalism career, she taught in an underresourced school in Louisiana through the AmeriCorps Teach for America program.

Tracy holds a master's degree in English literature from Boston College and a B.A. in the same from St. Mary's University. When she's not writing, she likes to scuba dive, forget to go to kickboxing class, wallow in bed with a good book or get out her new guitar with a group of friends and pretend she's Suzanne Vega.

She loves to hear from readers—e-mail TracyMontoya@aol.com or visit www.tracymontoya.com.

Books by Tracy Montoya

CAST OF CHARACTERS

Sabrina Adelante—Port Renegade National Park's lead search-and-rescue tracker, Sabrina has long carried Rosie Donovan's disappearance on her conscience because she had to call off the search when it reached a dead end.

Aaron Donovan—The police detective knows in his gut that his missing daughter is still alive, and he'll do anything to find her.

Rosie Donovan—The daughter of Aaron Donovan who went missing while hiking in Renegade Ridge State Park six months ago.

Tara Fisher—When the Port Renegade High School student disappears while hiking, Sabrina and Aaron wonder if it might be connected to Rosie.

Jessie DiCosta and Alex Gray—The other two members of Sabrina's tracking team, Jessie and Alex are also her good friends.

Skylar Jones—The liaison between the Park Rangers and the search-and-rescue trackers, Skylar is responsible for coordinating searches for people missing inside the Park.

Eddie Ventaglia—Aaron's partner on the police force, Eddie is also Rosie's godfather—and he holds a grudge against Sabrina for calling off the search for her.

Mary Beth Peterson—A "floating" psychiatrist who serves the Port Renegade Police department, Mary Beth won't let Aaron disappear into his grief.

The Overman—A predator who's behind the disappearances of at least three young women from Port Renegade State Park.

Chapter One

Sabrina Adelante's sturdy Casio Pathfinder watch beeped once on the hour, the shrill noise causing her skin to prickle with restless anxiety.

Time was working against one very young and very lost girl, and even her watch had something to say about that.

Time, and some idiot at the Port Renegade PD. Tara Fisher had been missing for nearly two hours inside the state park. Two hours before the police had thought to call in the park search-and-rescue unit—never mind that the hiking trails on which Tara had disappeared were as familiar as breathing to every member of the SAR team. Two hours during which Tara, walking at an average pace, could cover about five miles.

Given that Tara could have traveled in

any direction from point last seen, or PLS, their search area was a circle with a radius of five miles and, as any geometry student could tell you, an overall area of nearly eighty miles.

Damn the Port Renegade Police to hell.

With a snap of her wrist, Sabrina wrenched the steering wheel to the right, executing a too-quick turn into the parking area at the Black Wolf Run trailhead and sending a spray of gravel into the air. She barely registered the sound of tiny stones raining against her shiny black paint job as she stomped on the brake, bringing the car to a skidding halt.

Muttering a few Spanish curses that years ago would have had her mother stuffing a bar of soap in her mouth, Sabrina angrily kicked open the Jeep's door. As she stepped out, Alex Gray and Jessie DiCosta, the other two members of her tracking team, jogged across the parking lot to greet her. She gave them a quick nod of acknowledgment as she hefted her bulging backpack in front of her to rummage through it.

When the two of them reached the Jeep, Alex reached inside its open back to pull her walking stick out, just as he had a hundred times before. "Here you go, beautiful." Holding the stick out with one hand, he used the other to readjust the backward Mariners baseball cap that had already flattened his short, dark hair. He wore the thing so often, it was a wonder it hadn't fused to his head.

She glared at him while leaning her body against the driver's-side door until it closed with a heavy click. Normally she would have laughed or at least snorted at the "beautiful"—her mom had always said Alex would flirt with a broom in a dress if one presented himself. Today, she merely smacked the sheet of paper she'd dug out of her pack against his chest, leaving him scrambling to grab it when she let go. She tucked her stick under her arm and then handed a second sheet to Jessie, who'd been quietly waiting beside her.

And then her skin started to prickle and crawl with the peculiar kind of restlessness that her family generally referred to as "ants-in-her-pants syndrome." Whatever they wanted to call it, all she knew was that her body needed to be in motion, because standing still in the parking lot had suddenly become unbearable. Knowing

Jess and Alex would understand, Sabrina pulled her pack onto her shoulders and started off toward the trailhead without another word.

A few seconds later, Jessie came up beside her, her long, athletic legs matching Sabrina's stride for stride and then some. She reached out with one pale, freckle-dotted hand and untwisted one of the shoulder straps of Sabrina's backpack as they walked. "Jacket?" She motioned with her head back toward the Jeep, then caught her shoulder-length blond hair in her hands, tying it up with a rubber band into a messy knot. "Smells like rain."

Sabrina slanted a glance at Jess and kept moving, her hiking boots crunching down hard on the gravel as she headed toward where the trailhead sat enshrouded by a thick cluster of hemlock and giant sequoias. "Screw the jacket," she said, then immediately regretted her harsh tone. While she didn't mean to direct her anger at Jessie, she knew her tracking partner well enough to know that her colleague's sweet nature also came with a highly sensitive side. "But thank you," she added.

Alex whistled as he jogged up to take his

place on Sabrina's other side. "Damn, you're tense today. Whaddup, boss?"

"We're looking for Tara Fisher." All three of them were finally on the move, but that fact did little to settle the butterflies of anxiety knocking against Sabrina's rib cage. "Senior at Port Renegade High. She's five foot one, weighs 110 pounds, and is wearing a navy-blue zip-up sweatshirt and jeans. Her point last seen is Hot Spring Seven, which is where she and her friend Paula Rivers were soaking when she decided to try to find a sweet spot on the mountain where her cell phone might work. Paula said she waited about twenty minutes and then tried to look for Tara, but she never found her."

Hot Spring Seven was one of at least twenty hot-spring pools along Black Wolf Run, an intermediate five-mile hiking trail that wound up the first third of Renegade Ridge, through what was arguably one of Washington state's most beautiful forests. The springs—some hidden, others out in plain view—were what made Black Wolf Run one of the more popular trails in the whole fourteen hundred square miles of Renegade Ridge State Park. Despite the unpredictable terrain in the park, visitors rarely got lost on or near Black Wolf, as it was pretty straightforward—go straight up, soak in a spring, come straight down. But that's not to say Tara couldn't have wandered off the path or jumped onto another trail in the weblike network that wound through the park.

"Who reported her missing?" Jessie asked as they moved into the cool, damp shade of the forest canopy. Almost as if they'd choreographed it, Jessie and Alex fell back about five feet and fanned out behind her. Sabrina was the point person of their SAR team—the one who would follow the girls' trail, step-by-step. As flank trackers, Jessie and Alex's job was to look forward while Sabrina looked at the ground, shouting out warnings when another set of tracks was about to intersect the ones they were following, or when Sabrina might be about to run into a tree or a person.

"Paula bypassed the ranger station and called the police as soon as she came down the mountain," Sabrina said.

To Sabrina's left, Alex muttered a soft curse under his breath, letting her know she didn't have to explain any further. She did anyway. "The police, in turn, bumbled around from two-thirty to four before calling us. Add twenty minutes for us all to get here and for the tracking team leaders to get briefed, and you have…"

She let the sentence trail off. All three of them knew what they had. They had a lost, undoubtedly frightened girl who'd been missing for way too long. The first few hours were critical when it came to finding a lost hiker.

Her walking stick struck packed dirt with a frustrated thump as the gravel portion of the trail ended, and the sounds of Alex's and Jessie's followed. It only took them seconds to reach the bend in the trail, where the ferns lining the side of the gravel path marched inward, narrowing the passage on Black Wolf Run. Tall, densely-packed coniferous trees—mostly Douglas firs, Sitka spruce and the western hemlocks that marked the area as temperate rainforest—also closed in around them, dripping with moss and blocking out much of the pale-gray light overhead.

"Two hours." Jessie sighed. "What is the matter with these people?"

If they were lucky, Tara would be sitting

on a rock somewhere, waiting for them. But as they'd all learned from experience, teenagers rarely held still, especially when caught up in a panic.

A flurry of footprints that looked like the right size caught her eye, and Sabrina stopped to examine them. Crouching near the loose dirt dusting the edge of the trail, she scanned the area, piecing together a complete print in her mind from the partials before her.

The muffled sound of thunder rumbled from the east, and she glanced upward at the fast-rolling gray clouds, the fall breeze that drove them sending a chill across her exposed face and hands. This part of the Olympic Mountain Range, in a region where southern maritime and northern outflow winds combined, was known for bad weather and heavy precipitation—both of which would undoubtedly strike before the afternoon was over.

Jessie crouched down beside her, careful to stay back out of her line of sight. "Those papers you gave us, that was Tara's footprint, right?" She tugged the sheet out of her pants pocket and unfolded it, examining the footprint image on it once more.

"Not exactly," Sabrina replied. "And these

aren't the ones we're looking for." She stood, dusting her hands off on her pants leg.

"Nope," Alex concurred from her other side as he and Jessie rose as well. "Close, though."

Leaning over, she traced the footprint on Jessie's sheet of paper with her finger. "This image is actually of the friend's boot. Paula and Tara like to shop together, so they bought the same brand of hiking boots on the same day from the same store. Tara's are size-six Ecco brand hiking boots with a hexagonal lug print. Paula's about your height, so…."

"So Paula has monster feet, as evidenced by what's on this paper, and Miss 110-Pounds has the very tiny version," the six-foot-one Jessie finished with a wry smile. As usual, Sabrina was surprised at Jessie's self-deprecating comment. The woman was all lean muscle with a dancer's grace, and that, coupled with her long blond hair and freckled complexion, gave her the wholesome look of an outdoor-gear model.

"You have very nice feet," Alex said, wagging his dark eyebrows at her. "Nothing monster about them."

"I bet you say that to all the girls," Jessie returned in a bored, exaggerated monotone, more than used to Alex's flirtatious ways.

Sabrina barely registered the conversation. She could still feel Paula's hand clutching her arm. *Something's wrong. Tara's scared to death of hiking by herself. She'd never disappear like this.*

Not that she hadn't heard those words a hundred times before, but still... Sabrina couldn't shake the feeling that despite her SAR team's excellent record when it came to finding the missing, today wasn't going to be their lucky day. Call it intuition, call it her reaction to the smell of storms in the air. It felt too much like the day Rosie Donovan went missing, the day the police started their vendetta against everyone on the park's search-and-rescue team because of her.

Don't think about Rosie.

The sound of a polite cough accomplished what her mind couldn't, drawing her attention to Jessie, who shifted her lanky frame from side to side, obviously itching to get going again. She'd been a star basketball player at the University of Washington, so sometimes when she grew impatient she'd get a look about her as though she was about to swat you to the side and go for a layup.

Grabbing her radio off her belt, Sabrina pressed the talk button down with her thumb. "Base, this is Tracker One," she said into it. "We've passed the trailhead and are heading to the PLS. I need someone up here to close off this trail, stat, over." She lifted her thumb off the button.

"Tracker One, there's a park ranger on her way. Should be there in two minutes, over." A spectacular burst of static punctuated the end of Skylar Jones's statement. Skylar was the site coordinator, the one who briefed tracking teams and dispatched them when someone went missing inside the park. Several months ago, Sabrina had had her job, but she'd quickly demoted herself back to lead tracker shortly thereafter. Being cooped up in the ranger station while everyone else hit the trails was not her idea of a satisfying workday.

Alex moved up next to Sabrina, squinting down the trail. Just after taking a sharp bend to the right, a series of switchbacks climbed up the steep initial portion, and then it was a fairly moderate climb to the hot springs. "You okay, Bree?"

Tara's scared to death....

Blinking out of her thoughts, she turned to look at Alex. His close-cropped dark hair, mostly hidden today under the Mariners ball cap, held not a trace of gray, and very few lines marred skin that seemed to stay perpetually tan, despite Port Renegade's infamous lack of sunshine. Other than not sporting the permed mullet that had been all the rage back in the day, Alex looked exactly the same as he had when they'd graduated from high school together. "I'm fine," Sabrina said, as the ants in her pants kicked in in a big, bad way. She started walking.

"Yes, you are fine." Alex bared his teeth at her in a vulpine grin.

Sabrina rolled her eyes and kept moving, the two flank trackers following suit.

Alex sighed. "Ah, come on, Bree. You know you want me."

"Gross. You're like a brother. Knock it off and get back there."

"We'll find her, Bree. At least, if someone can stop sexually harassing his tracking partners for two minutes and concentrate." Jessie widened her eyes and pursed her lips at Alex, then fell back herself and moved to the outer edge of the trail on Sabrina's right. "We always find them."

Normally Alex would have pretended to take offense to the harassment comment, but this time, he was quiet, and Sabrina found his silence unnerving as she turned her eyes back to the ground. "Not always," he finally murmured.

Usually, you couldn't beat the positive out of the man with a stick, but maybe he, too, felt something was different about today's search. Though they didn't like to talk about the ones they found too late, they were always in their minds on every search. And six months ago, there had been one they hadn't found at all….

They moved slowly along the edge of the trail, walking perpendicular to the footprints on the ground, searching for the sets that would signify that Paula and Tara's Ecco hiking boots had put their stamp on the ground. They hadn't even made it to the switchbacks before Sabrina found the telltale hexagonal lug pattern of Tara's size-sixes, and Paula's larger prints were right beside them. Bending down, she once again slipped out of the backpack's shoulder straps, setting the bag on the ground and fishing out a piece of sturdy wire and some crepe paper.

"Nice work," Jessie said, once more holding out the copy of the footprint they'd made from Paula's boot back at the ranger station for comparison.

"Easy enough in the middle of the afternoon," Sabrina replied, bending a piece of wire and tying a bit of crepe paper to the end to make a miniature stake to mark the tracks. Sticking the tiny flag into the ground next to one of the prints, Sabrina rose, pulling her radio to her mouth as she did so.

"Base, this is Tracker One. We've IDed the trail and are continuing to the PLS, over," she said.

"Roger that, Tracker One. Over," came the reply.

With the trail found and freshly laid, Sabrina didn't have too much trouble following it—especially since they knew it was heading toward Hot Spring Seven. It was very rare to find non-locals who'd discovered number seven—well-hidden as it was by lush ferns and the tangled roots of an ancient moss-covered Douglas fir. The girls were local, and they knew these trails well.

But that fact didn't make the thought of

Tara leaving her friend any less strange, given that the girl was allegedly afraid of hiking alone.

Eyes on the ground, Adelante.

The three reached the spring within an hour, jogging on the flat parts of the path, walking as quickly as they could with the aid of their walking sticks on the switchbacks and steeper inclines. Because they knew where Tara had ended up, they'd had the luxury of speeding up the trail instead of searching out every last print, even though the smooth-soled prints had intersected with and rubbed out the girls' tracks every so often. Just before they reached the spring, Sabrina slowed their pace. Fortunately, it was easy to see that no one else had been to this particular spring recently, as there were quite a few to choose from, so they wouldn't be dealing with any other tracks on the grass.

"Looks like they stopped right here." Jessie pointed to the cluster of telltale heel curves, smooth spots, and dislodged pebbles in a patch of dirt around the steaming waters of the spring. "They probably hung their clothes in these branches." With an impatient flick of her hand, she brushed her ponytail behind her, then patted a low-hanging branch that hit her at waist level. "Took off their shoes here and slipped in." She pointed to several overlapping prints, made by booted and bare feet.

All business now, Alex took off his cap and ran his hand through his hair, then jammed the hat back on his head, never taking his eyes off the ground. "We know that Tara got out of the spring before Paula did, saying she had to make a call on her cell phone. So where did she exit?"

Sabrina scanned the edges of the clear pool, the soft, mineral-packed mud at its bottom long settled after the girls' departure. A few tiny bubbles surfaced from the bottom, as Mother Nature piped in steaming water from an underground river.

"There," she said finally. Though it wasn't a full print, Sabrina could clearly see a flat spot in the dirt, on the other side of the spring just behind the Douglas fir's rough trunk. Pretty much the only things in nature that created flat spots like that were humans and hooved animals, and she didn't think any hooved animals had decided to climb the ridge and go for a dip today.

Grabbing a low-hanging branch, Sabrina negotiated her way around the spring and moved into point once more, Jessie and Alex falling into place behind her. She marked the first print with one of her wire-and-tissue-paper stakes, and then followed Tara's tracks, which ran along the side of the ridge.

She could see where Tara had stopped in the pine-needle-strewn dirt, obviously shifting her weight around as she'd tried to use her phone, and then, for some reason, the girl had continued forward, starting to snake upwards as well toward a break in the trees up ahead. When Sabrina and her team reached the break, they spilled out into a small, grassy clearing.

"Trail intersecting about fifteen feet ahead, coming from above," Alex called out. Sabrina took her eyes off the ground.

With their years of experience, tracking in grass was as easy as tracking in dirt. You just had to know what to look for. And the still-flattened line in the grass practically screamed at her that another person had been here, too. But whether that person had come down the mountain at the same time Tara was wandering up remained to be seen.

Turning her attention back to the trail, Sabrina moved forward once more, finding and following every place where Tara's feet had left a spot of bent grass or broken and bruised plants.

"Trail intersection coming up," Jessie called.

Sure enough, the line of crushed greenery came into her field of vision with her next step.

Sabrina came to an abrupt halt. Behind her, Jessie blew out a noisy breath. "Bree? Oh, no."

She felt the two flank trackers move in beside her, as they, too, took in and interpreted the tracks on the ground. A thick silence descended as they all studied the chaotic sign once, twice, three times. Sabrina knew they were all probably hoping that one of the team would speak up, reassuring the others with a benign interpretation of what lay before them. The reassurance never came.

In her peripheral vision, Sabrina saw Jessie bend to pick up something in the grass. Jessie held it out to her, and Sabrina's fingers closed on a cell phone.

Not again. Please, God.

Behind her, she barely registered when Alex radioed the base and told Skylar to call 911.

"Roger that," the staticky voice replied. "Cops are on their way."

And all Sabrina could think was, *Too late*.

TARA AWOKE to a sharp pain piercing her between the shoulder blades.

Ow. Not fun.

She felt groggy, sluggish. Like she'd just stayed up studying all night for a test. And her arms hurt.

Lolling her head around to loosen the tight muscles in her neck, she tried to relax, to go back to sleep. But her body hurt all over, and her head was pounding. And she was so cold. Had Dad turned the heat down again to save money on the electric bill? Drove her nuts when he did that. She felt like she was ninety years old when she woke up freezing like this, every joint creaking and groaning in protest when she rolled out of bed.

But she wasn't in bed. She felt like she was standing.

Weird.

Too disturbed by the unfamiliarity of her situation to go back to sleep, Tara struggled to open her eyes. But for some reason, they wouldn't cooperate. So she flexed her shoulders and brought her arms down to her sides.

Or tried to.

A faint rattle was her only reward. Her hands stayed firmly above her head, pinned by something clinging to her wrists. She pulled her arms downward again, causing the pain in her upper back to radiate throughout her body.

What the heck?

Some kind of crust seemed to have formed on her eyes, like the kind that made your lashes stick together when you'd forgotten to take off your mascara at night. But this felt stickier, like mascara times seven, and it had gunked her eyes completely shut. And her head hurt like nobody's business.

Once again, she tried to bring her hands down, to wipe away the crud on her face and stretch her aching muscles.

Nothing. Just that sound again.

The fuzziness of sleep left her abruptly as adrenaline shot through her system. That man.

Her arms jerked involuntarily at the memory of the figure coming down the mountain toward her, quick and stealthy, like a stalking panther. Tara's heart started to pound, in time with the pulsing ache in her head. She jerked her arms again, once more noticing the rattle that accompanied the movement. The move itself had set her off balance, and her body twirled slightly to the left, leaving her torso twisted and balanced on her toes like some freakish ballerina. Cold metal dug into her wrists, and the pain between her shoulder blades grew more excruciating as she fought to right herself, her bare toes barely coming into contact with what felt like a cold, concrete floor. God, what was happening to her?

Her breathing quickened, and she felt the first traces of panic creeping down her spine like a pointy-legged spider. Tears leaked out of her closed eyes, loosening things enough that she was finally able to pull one open. She could feel the gunk on her lashes against her cheek every time she blinked, waiting to adjust her vision to a brightness that never came.

Pitch black.

That's when the reality of her situation hit her.

She was alone, in a dark, dark room with her arms chained above her head.

And she was naked.

The chains rattled again as her hands involuntarily jerked down to cover her bare body, though of course, that proved impossible. Her skin prickled into painful goose-flesh from the damp, unrelenting cold that surrounded her, and try as she might, she couldn't make out even the most indistinct shapes around her.

Alone in the dark. With only the sound of her teeth chattering to keep her company.

Mommy?

Tara was seventeen years old, far too old to address her mother that way, but she would have given anything to hear her mother's voice calling, feel her mom's soft arms around her, taking off the chains, rubbing the soreness from her shoulders.

A soft whimper escaped her. She thought she heard a low sigh in response. A male sound. A sound of satisfaction.

Mommy?   Mommymommymommy-mommymommy!

She didn't realize she'd spoken out loud until she heard him laughing.

Her body jolted again, sending her spinning to face the sound. "Who are you?" she cried. "What the hell are you, some kind of freak?"

He must have moved, because this time, the laughter came from behind her. She turned again to face him, her bare toes scrambling for purchase on the icy floor. She felt something warm running down her cheeks and realized that she was still crying. It was all coming back to her—the hike to the hot springs with Paula, the way the warm water had felt on her aching feet, the shadow on the rocks, the tall, thin stranger standing above her. She'd tried to speak to him, to say hello, but he'd grabbed her, she'd tried to escape, and then everything had gone black.

He was still laughing. A slow fury boiled up inside her, and she clenched her hands—still stretched above her head—until her fingernails dug painfully into her palms.

"What do you want?"

In response, she heard a small click, and then a brilliant, blinding light assaulted her eyes like an explosion. She turned her head abruptly to the side, squeezing her eyelids shut. She didn't want to see. She wanted to wake up and find out that this was all just a dream, not real, not this. But after a few seconds of silence, she couldn't stand it anymore and peered into the brightness, blinking rapidly as her eyesight adjusted.

He was standing in front of a spotlight— the large, portable kind the police sometimes used at crime scenes on TV—lighting a cigarette. The acrid smell of tobacco smoke wafted toward her, and she realized he could see her naked. Then, almost simultaneously, Tara realized that his seeing her was the least of her worries.

At that point, a horrible feeling prickled across her skin, causing her teeth to chatter again, making her whole body tremble and strain against the chains. She wasn't going to see her mother, not ever again. Not Paula, not her school, not her boyfriend Todd, the captain of the soccer team in a football town. Just this horrible place, with this man whose refusal to speak terrified her more than anything.

"What do you want?" she asked, her voice a small, shaking thing, knowing as she asked that he wouldn't answer.

He took the cigarette from his lips and smiled. They stared at each other for a long time. And then he finally moved, putting one hand on the back of her neck, the other moving to encircle her waist. Overcome by the urge to throw up, Tara still managed not to scream. Not until she felt him crush his cigarette out on the vulnerable skin at the small of her back.

Chapter Two

As they followed the teenager's path to its conclusion, Sabrina could practically hear the giant clock in her head ticking the precious seconds away. The sad thing was that even though she was rushing her team down the mountain, she knew they'd never make up those lost hours—and it would be Tara who paid for it.

"Hold up a minute." She stopped and braced herself with a hand against the rough bark of a pine tree. It was always a bad sign when the mixture of dry pine needles and damp dirt and grass on the ground began to blur, the images smashing together as if someone had put pieces of the forest into a kaleidoscope.

"You want me on point, Bree?" Jessie asked, crunching to a halt behind her.

Sabrina shook her head, and God bless America, her vision cleared once more. "No. No, I'm okay. Just lost the tracks for a minute." She reached up to rub the bridge of her nose, then dropped her hand to scan the ground. It only took a few seconds to find where Tara's trail converged with someone else's—a male who'd left large prints, about a size eleven or so, with a thick zigzag pattern on the sole. But then something odd happened—Tara's prints vanished, and the man's continued, bearing telltale scuff marks at the toes, which told them he may have been carrying something heavy. Like a teenaged girl.

She didn't even want to think about why Tara may have needed to be carried.

They pushed on, until finally, the trees started to thin to the point where the green, wet dimness that had enveloped them all the way down the mountain gave way to stretches of gray sky that provided only a little more illumination. Eventually, with an abruptness that Sabrina had always found a little shocking, nature ran into human construction as the team spilled out onto a slim, gravel-packed logging road. The trees, of course, stopped at the road's edge.

Unfortunately, so did the tracks.

"Take a rest, Bree," Jessie said as she moved up beside Sabrina. "You've been on point for a while now. Alex and I will check the roadsides, and we can switch positions once we find the trail again."

If we find the trail again. Blowing upward so her sideswept bangs lifted slightly off her forehead, Sabrina just nodded, refusing to give a voice to her doubts. She reached up to rub the back of her neck, feeling the fatigue starting to creep into her muscles now that she wasn't moving. Alex and Jessie spread out and started cutting for sign—searching for telltale indicators that they'd found the continuation of the trail— along the sides of the road. Sabrina let her hand drop, and she knew, she *knew* her flank trackers wouldn't find anything. She'd noticed the tire tracks the minute they'd set foot on the logging road— noticed, but hadn't wanted to confront the truth they told.

He'd parked his car here. And with the small amount of traffic that came through this way, it would be a miracle if anyone had seen it—or him. Or Tara.

Here's a riddle for you: How can you make a girl vanish in the forest so the state's best trackers can't find her?

Wrap her up and get her out on a vehicle—car, four-wheeler, dirt bike. Wrap her up. Get her out. Hide until we stop looking.

Feeling a headache coming on, Sabrina rolled her head around, trying to drive out some of the tension settling at the base of her neck and smack in the middle of her right temple. The gray sky suddenly grew brighter, so bright that it almost hurt to keep her eyes open. She ducked her head, looking at the small pools of moisture that had formed in dips in the gravel. She caught one at just the right angle, and it glowed, reflecting the sky and sending a sharp bolt of pain through her right temple.

Oh, hell. Hell, hell, hell. All signs pointed to her having about an hour before the migraine really hit, and after that, she'd be more useless than a paper hat in a rainstorm. She shoved her hand into the cargo pocket on the side of her leg, checking for the bottle of ibuprofen she always carried. It didn't always help, but sometimes, if she swallowed at least four of the little orange pills in time, she could head off the worst of it.

Sometimes.

Please, let them work this time. Tara needed her.

Or maybe Sabrina needed to look for Tara. It didn't matter. What mattered was that they not give up, that they find the man who snatched her off the mountain. That they find *her.*

Don't think about what condition she'd be in when they found her. Don't think.

Pressing the pills to her mouth, Sabrina swallowed them dry, their hard edges scraping the inside of her throat. She reached up to pull at the rubber band that was holding her hair in place. Keeping her heavy, black hair out of her eyes was always a plus on the job, but at that moment, the ponytail just made her scalp ache. As her hair fell around her shoulders, doing nothing to ease the pain in her head, she heard the slow crunch of tires on gravel. Pulling the rubber band around her wrist, she turned to see an unmarked police cruiser crawl slowly through the mist. The brown sedan slowed to a halt several yards away, and that's when she finally noticed that a thin yet relentless drizzle had coated her arms and face—the trees had probably protected the team from it while they had been under their cover.

Though it was an unmarked vehicle, it had one of those bubble lights resting precariously on the roof, as if the driver had tossed it up there in a hurry. Her head started to throb in time with the flashing red light as it broke up the gray and green of their surroundings. She could just make out the silhouette of the lone driver behind the windshield whenever the wipers pushed the mist out of the way for a moment. The driver turned the engine off, but he didn't get out.

Whatever.

Wrapping her arms around her body, Sabrina tried to ignore her growing discomfort. She had a job to do, and if some lazy cop was afraid of getting a little wet, so be it. After setting her bag on the damp ground, she opened it and pulled out a small piece of waterproof tarp. Crouching down next to the backpack, she used rocks to make a little tent with the tarp over a portion of the tire track. That would preserve most of the track if it started to rain hard, and the cops could cast it at their leisure—which apparently they had a lot of, since the officer behind her still hadn't come out of his car. She got a small camera out of the pack and took a few flash pictures, just in case.

At the sound of a car door finally slamming behind her, Sabrina stood, her back still to their visitor, and tossed the camera back in her bag. Her head throbbing in time with her suddenly racing pulse, she shoved her damp hair out of her eyes, then twisted it into a loose, wet braid. God, telling the cop what they'd discovered was not going to be easy. Because someone had gone missing on Renegade Ridge, and for the second time, Sabrina had no clues left on how to find her.

"Ms. Adelante."

She was just about to tell the speaker that Ms. Adelante was her mother and to call her Sabrina, when something about his low baritone struck her as familiar. She closed her eyes, just for a moment, wishing hard that the cop would be a stranger. Then she turned, knowing before she saw his face exactly who he was.

"Aaron." His name came out almost on a sigh.

The drizzle was growing heavier, and it

coated Aaron Donovan's tousled, slightly too-long brown hair with shiny droplets. His eyes were set so deep, Jessie had once commented that they always seemed to either be glaring at you or using their X-ray powers to look at your bones. They were fixated on her at the moment, and she had no doubt Aaron was glaring today. The thin jacket he wore over his black dress pants and gray shirt and tie was already soaked through, but he didn't seem to feel the cold.

"Storm coming," he said when he reached her, and there were a thousand unspoken words contained within that one phrase. Aaron Donovan stole her breath, and not just because of his physical presence.

The detective's deep voice sounded calm, reasonable, almost as if he were informing her that her car was parked in a disabled spot or that she'd just jaywalked across Main Street. But beneath that calm was a man ready to snap—and she knew that he'd long ago marked her as the reason. It was in the restlessness that hummed off his body, the mix of anger and steely resolve still in his expression. And to tell the truth, it scared her.

"Yes, Detective, there's a storm coming,"

she said, proud of herself for keeping her voice strong and calm, despite the fact that every muscle in her body was so tense, she thought she might break into a million pieces at the slightest touch. Not that he would ever think of touching her.

They stared at each other, the thousand unsaid words still hanging between them, a thousand accusations in Aaron Donovan's still, gray eyes. It was Sabrina who turned away first, looking up to where wispy, almost-black clouds were rapidly rolling underneath the overcast sky, pushed along by a wind that was getting stronger by the minute.

"How long are you going to keep up the search?" he asked quietly.

The search had just started. It was an inappropriate question, and he knew it.

Don't break down. Don't cry. Don't show that female weakness—you can't afford it. Sabrina took a moment just to breathe, to get control of the swirl of emotions threatening to make her lose it completely. "As long as we can," she finally replied, her eyes still turned up to the sky. She knew he wanted to hear the words "as long as it takes" come out of her mouth, but that was one promise she'd broken before. She'd never make it again, especially not to him. "But I need to tell you—" God, she didn't want to tell him they'd lost another young girl. Not him. She didn't think she could stand to see that blame in his eyes again.

I had no choice, you son of a bitch. Get out of my head.

"Your department took two hours to call us out here," she snapped finally, looking him in the eye once more. "No one knows the parklands like we do. They should have called us in sooner."

And that's when he knew. He understood what she was about to tell him, and the knowledge drained the color from his face, his full, chiseled mouth growing even harder. One hand darted under his jacket, no doubt to find the gun tucked into a shoulder holster. But there was no one to threaten. No one to shoot. Tara had vanished, and so had the man who'd met her on the ridge, leaving a chilling story told in footprints behind them.

"Not again," he finally managed, sounding as if he would choke on the words.

Without thinking, she reached for him, just to put a hand on his arm, to offer some comfort. With a barely audible hiss, he moved out of her reach, so her fingers only grazed his sleeve. And then they could only stare at each other.

Sabrina broke the silence when she couldn't stand it anymore. "Cast this tire track. I think it's important." His face darkened for a moment, and then he gave her a curt nod, reaching for his own radio. It only took him a minute to mobilize the department crime scene techs, asking them to come out to the ridge with some dental stone as soon as possible. The drizzle wouldn't harm the track for a while, but full-fledged rain would.

"Bree?" Behind her, she heard Alex crunching down on the gravel road.

"Wha—?" God, she hoped she'd been wrong about the car. She hoped they had discovered something she'd missed.

"You'll want to see what we found," Alex continued, addressing Aaron this time. "I can show you."

Ah, so Alex was rescuing her from the big, bad detective. And heaven help her, she wanted to be rescued.

Stealing a glance at Aaron, who'd since gotten off his radio, she saw the corner of his hard mouth twitch upward, giving a slightly mocking edge to his expression. Guess he knew just how much she wanted to run away from him. But it was important that one of them take the police up to the clearing—it was a crime scene, after all, and she well knew that looking for miniscule evidence was hardly SAR's area of expertise.

"No, Alex, it's okay. I'll take him up." She immediately wanted to kick herself for the perverse stubbornness that made her refuse Alex's tacit offer just because of a slight challenge in the cop's eyes that she may or may not have imagined. Trudge up the mountain alone with Aaron Donovan? Now, *that* was going to be a real kick in the head. But it was too late for her to back down now, and they all knew it. "See what Jessie wants and then call in the team that was dispatched along these logging roads. If the trail does pick up again, we'll need as many bodies as we can to help us find it."

The tire tracks flashed once more in her mind. They weren't going to find a thing.

As Alex started to turn away, she spoke again. "Alex, make sure you protect this tire print."

Widening his eyes, Alex scrutinized the track, then looked at her questioningly.

"Until the crime scene people get here to cast it. It might be important." With a nod, he moved toward Jessie, leaving Sabrina alone with Aaron.

She looked him straight in the eye, refusing to flinch even though it took all she had. "Come on." With that, Sabrina took off, darting into the trees and moving swiftly and silently up the ridge. Now that she knew where the footprints lay, she had no trouble following them back up.

Given that her job entailed a lot of hiking, not to mention rock climbing and rappelling, Sabrina was in excellent shape, despite the fact that no amount of extra sit-ups would give her the six-pack abs Jessie and Alex had. So hiking up this rather benign part of the mountain without a trail wasn't that much of a challenge, even though it would have had most people huffing and puffing. But damn if Aaron wasn't keeping up. Actually, he wasn't just keeping up, he was snapping at her heels like a pack of wild dogs, pushing her farther and faster.

In less than half an hour, they reached the spot where Sabrina had seen the last of Tara's footprints, not a word having passed between them. Careful not to disturb the trail, she motioned to the detective to follow directly behind her, leading them both to where Tara's trail first led away from the hot spring.

"Paula said she stayed behind soaking in the pool while Tara went out to make a call on her cell phone," Sabrina explained, even though she knew Aaron had probably learned that bit of information two hours before she had. Not that she was bitter. "You can see the lug print of her hiking boots here." She pointed to the trail, and Aaron nodded, scanning the ground. She walked him to the clearing where Jessie and Alex had first spotted the man's trail intersecting with Tara's.

"So, there's the mystery trail, made by someone we believe was on the mountain at the same time as the girls," she continued, gesturing to the line of crushed grass that still remained, although it had grown fainter as the grass healed itself and began to stand up again. "It looks like he met up with Tara."

Okay, now his silence was really getting to her. She stopped walking and waited for him to respond, noticing that he was staring at the ground as if he could interpret the signs himself. But she knew that wasn't the case.

"These tracks were made at the same time as Tara's?" he asked. He wasn't questioning her, just asking for an explanation. For which she should probably be grateful, given their past.

She took a couple of steps to where the ground erupted in a sudden confusion of broken weeds and plants and disturbed dirt in a language that was completely foreign to him, but plain as day to her. "Look over here." She crouched down by the prints and moved her hand above the ground to show him what she was talking about. "She stopped to talk to him. You can tell by the number of prints overlapping and shuffling here. People don't hold still when they talk to each other— they're always moving, shifting their weight."

"You know the prints are male by the size?" he asked quietly, choosing to tower above her rather than join her on the ground. The jerk.

"That, and the fact that they point

outward—men tend to do that, while most women turn their toes slightly inward." It was a delaying tactic, that explanation. She didn't want to show him what they'd seen next.

"I know there's something you don't want to tell me, but we'll be up here all night unless you step it up."

All night, alone with Aaron Donovan. Once upon a time, that might have been an appealing proposition. Now, it just made her head hurt. She reached up to rub the bridge of her nose, a soft "ahh" of pain escaping her lips before she could stop it.

He was by her side in a heartbeat, crouched before her so his too-handsome face was directly in hers. "Are you all right?" His hand curved around her bicep, as if to offer comfort, though it hovered inches above her skin.

She reared back, shocked at his question, at the notion that he might care even slightly about her answer.

"Sabrina?"

Pushing off the ground with her hands, she sprang to her feet, smacking her palms together to clean off the pine needles that had clung to her skin. "I wasn't the one who waited for two hours before calling us in, Detective," she replied, practically spitting out the title as she dusted her hands on the front of her pants. He rose slowly and lifted an eyebrow in response, the mocking look back on his face.

Shaken and not really knowing why, Sabrina spun away from him. She had no time for this—on that point, Donovan was right. She needed to step it up for Tara. With an impatient motion of her hand, she indicated for Aaron to follow her, not looking at him as she led the way to the next patch of dirt that had a couple of telltale hexagons embedded in it. Just ahead, she knew, were a few more complete versions of Tara's prints. "Right here, Tara's stride interval increases," she said, her tone all business now. "That's the distance between her footprints. Basically, that means she started to run."

Aaron swore under his breath, a ridge forming between his dark eyebrows. Overhead, the sky darkened perceptibly, and the rumble of thunder from the east seemed to be coming closer.

Sabrina gestured with her chin to a spot up ahead, the quick movement reverberat-

ing throughout her skull. "He followed her.
I think she fell."

It had taken her team several painstaking
minutes to piece together the whole grim
story, but piece it together they had, and as
she led him back down to where they'd left
Jessie and Alex, Sabrina relayed it to the detective. Someone had been perched on a
rock above Hot Spring Seven, presumably
watching the girls as they'd soaked in the
pool. As soon as Tara had gotten out to make
her phone call, he'd started down the
mountain, intercepting her as she'd made it
to the clearing. There was a struggle, and
Tara broke free and started to run, only to
be tackled to the ground a few seconds later.
Somehow, her attacker had managed to
subdue her, and the heavy, scuffing partial
prints they'd found as they made their way
down the mountain indicated that he'd
carried her down.

To the old logging road where his car
had sat, waiting for them.

He didn't say anything once she'd
finished. He pulled out his radio and
directed more police and the department
crime scene techs up the mountain from
where they stood, telling them in no uncer-

tain terms that they needed to avoid stepping near the trail of crepe-paper stakes she'd left behind. Once the first people started arriving, he'd offered to escort her back to the logging road in a tone that she knew was more demand than request.

Back at the road, she turned to him, meeting his gaze directly—and immediately wishing she hadn't. There was something so sad in his expression when you caught him off guard, just before he had a chance to close off again, a vulnerability that undid her more than his barely concealed hostility had.

"We have to find her," Aaron said simply, and because she knew what frightened him, his words made her ache for him.

Without thinking, she reached for him, her hand closing around his bare wrist. "Aaron," she said, because that's all she could say.

Gently, firmly, he pulled his arm away, the cool, collected cop once more. "I'll make sure someone casts that tire track," he said. "Thanks for your help, Ms. Adelante." Aaron turned and disappeared through the mist, heading toward his car.

As she watched him leave, the migraine

hit her full force, slamming into her skull like a freight train. Her vision blurred, and she stumbled, feeling rather pathetic as she caught herself by wrapping her arms around the rough bark of a sequoia. The clouds suddenly opened, and it started raining in sheets. The cold enveloped her, seeping into her very bones and causing her teeth to chatter.

"I'm all right," she murmured as she heard Jessie and Alex approach, willing herself to push away from the tree, to stand without support and keep looking. Her will wasn't enough.

She felt Jessie wrap something warm around her—probably her own all-weather jacket—and felt the woman's arms come around her. Sabrina couldn't see a damn thing. "Shh," Jessie said.

She heard them radio for help, and she closed her eyes, unable to deal with the piercing brightness of the sky.

"What did that man do to her?" Jessie asked Alex as she pulled the jacket's large hood over Sabrina's dripping hair.

"She gets migraines sometimes," Alex said. "Bad ones."

"Yeah, hello," Jessie retorted. "Alex, I saw her face when that detective was talking to her. What's his deal?"

Don't tell her. Don't say it. Sabrina didn't think she could stand to hear the words. The pain in her head sharpened, and she let herself lean against Jessie's sturdy frame.

Alex paused, probably weighing his words. "That was Detective Aaron Donovan."

Sabrina heard Jessie gasp.

"Yeah," Alex continued. "Rosie? That girl who went missing six months ago, around when you joined the staff? She was his daughter."

FRIEDRICH NIETZSCHE had introduced the concept of the *Übermensch,* which many lesser minds had erroneously translated to mean *superman.*" However, some scholars, himself included, knew that the German philosopher had meant *overman.* In other words, every human aspired—or should aspire—to become over-and-above Man, someone who transcends the crude limitations of humanity.

"I teach you the Overman," he pronounced

to the shivering mortals in his audience, knowing that they, too, should aspire to become like him, an *Übermensch*. But they wouldn't. They couldn't. It took a rare, special individual to overcome limitations and evolve into a superior being. But still, he couldn't give up. Still he had to try. "Man is something that shall be overcome. What have you done to overcome him?"

They scream, and they cry, and they refuse to see what lies before them.

"What have you done to overcome him?" he shouted back.

But they kept praying. And God was dead.

And in a universe where God was dead, he'd explained patiently, repeatedly, Man had to reconstruct himself, overcome the idea of himself as a fallen creature, slave to a moral code from on high. He has a responsibility to become something higher on the evolutionary scale. Ape created Man, and Man created Overman. And to get there, there could be no moral code. The Overman created his own moral code.

God was dead.

He took the whip from where it lay on a

shelf, wrapped it around the waist of a member of his audience. He pulled it to him, and it whimpered, a small, pathetic thing. He laughed, knowing that he could show it and the rest of his audience what it meant to be an Overman. His mouth pressed against its open, wailing one, and he gave it the breath, the very essence of himself, feeling the first stirrings of creation in his very core.

He pulled away. First, he had to continue the lesson. "Man is not becoming better simply by virtue of the passage of time," he told them. "We have to do something about it. Man can make himself better if he so chooses."

He traced the whip between a pair of ex-quisite breasts, quivering in anticipation. Beauty was the first requirement. Beauty begat physical strength begat super-intel-ligence begat…

The Overman. A race of Overmen.

Only he could have spirited his audience away. Only he had the intelligence, the ability to elude the mere mortals who lived below his mountain, trapped in mediocrity by their laws and their self-imposed limits.

They lived a certain way, thought a certain way, ate their dinners a certain way, never knowing what they had the potential to be, if only they would open their eyes. He would teach them, one by one. Like the Overmen before him—Magellan, Machiavelli, Napoleon, Caesar…even Hitler, in his twisted way—he would remake the world anew, into a brilliant, shining thing.

He walked behind his audience, the tremors of a new evolution taking control of him. It was his responsibility. He was the Overman. He'd won his own moral code. He would cleanse them and make them whole.

"We should be dissatisfied with ourselves," he said, his entire body shaking with the effort. "Without this dissatisfaction, there's no self- overcoming. No higher evolution of Man."

He brought the whip down, again and again, cleansing the blood of the new generation.

They scream, and they cry. Because God is dead.

Chapter Three

It's been two weeks....

No new sign...no new sign....

Her head felt as if someone had filled it with cement, thick and ponderous and nearly impossible to lift. She struggled to open her eyes.

Rosie's gone.

"Nooo." Pushing down with one arm, Sabrina propelled herself onto her back. Her eyelids fluttered open, and she saw a cup of steaming tea on her pale teak nightstand, smelled the cinnamon and herbs. Then, because keeping them open took too much effort, she let her eyes close once more.

The likelihood of her surviving up there isn't... I'm sorry....

Wake up. She had to wake up. Everything

just felt so…weighted, as though she had anchors tied to her limbs that were pulling her down, down under an ocean of still, quiet, dark water. She could hear the blood rushing in her ears, the thum-*thump* beat of her heart.

Two weeks.

Reaching up, she slowly dragged the back of her hand across her face, concentrating intensely on the movement so she wouldn't stop halfway and fall asleep again. So tired. With all of the effort it was taking to wake up fully, Sabrina considered just letting herself fall into unconsciousness again. Just for a little while.

Rosie's gone.

"Tara." The sharp memory of the missing girl suddenly gave Sabrina the strength to propel herself into a sitting position, the movement causing her head to spin ever so slightly.

"Whoa." The familiar deep voice came from her right, where a small, overstuffed chair sat tucked in the corner of the room. "Holy Bride of Frankenstein, that was sudden." She turned toward the voice and saw her brother Patricio sprawled in said chair.

"Rico, what the heck are you doing in my room?" The last vestiges of sleep abruptly disappeared from the surprise, and once her pulse went back to normal, Sabrina grinned, glad to see him despite her words. "How did you get in my house?"

His light brown eyes, the mirror image of her own—though he would have said his were the more masculine version—sparkled a bit as he relaxed back into the chair, looking rather smug and satisfied with himself. "I have my ways."

She rolled her eyes, and thank goodness, the movement didn't make her head throb anymore. "Okay, whatever." She quickly finger-combed her long hair. It was stick straight, so that small amount of effort was enough to get it to fall into place. Then, scrambling her way out of a pile of sheets, quilts and one puffy flowered comforter, she catapulted off the mattress and wrapped her arms around her brother. "I'm glad you're here."

He stood, lifting her off her feet in the process with an exaggerated grunt. She pretended to smack him on the head, after which he put her down, his broad hands still on her arms. "Me, too."

They'd found her less than a year ago, her three brothers. They'd all been separated when she was a baby, scattered by the California adoption system after the brutal murder of their parents. Thanks to a combination of bureaucratic red tape, a records-eating fire, and the machinations of their parents' killer, it had taken the siblings over twenty years to reunite. But from the moment she'd first seen Joe, Daniel and Patricio, Sabrina had felt instantly connected to them. And that feeling had never gone away, even though they were still separated by geography, she in Port Renegade, Washington, her brothers in Los Angeles.

"So when you moving to L.A., Bree?" Patricio asked as they walked out of her room and into her three-bedroom bungalow's sunny kitchen. Or, at least, it would have been sunny if it weren't raining all of the time. Having lived most of her life in Port Renegade with her adoptive parents and sister Casey, Sabrina found the rain comforting. Her oldest brother Joe hated it, Patricio's twin Daniel tolerated it and Patricio himself seemed neutral on the subject.

"Um, as soon as the Los Angeles Search and Rescue Team offers me a job. Because I'm sure my tracking skills would be in high demand in that concrete jungle, doofus." Shooting him a smile to soften the sarcasm, she reached up into one of her cupboards and brought down two coffee mugs, one with a caricature of Jane Austen on it, the other emblazoned with the logo of a save-the-forests nonprofit. "Coffee?" She'd taken a few appreciative sips of the tea Patricio had made for her, but coffee was her one true love in the morning.

"Sure." Patricio leaned his elbows on the breakfast bar in the middle of the room.

"What kind?"

He narrowed his eyes suspiciously at the silver-and-black espresso maker on her counter. "None of that stupid Seattle froufrou stuff. Just coffee. Black."

Sabrina pulled the machine toward her, twisting off the metal filter. She and Patricio went through this routine every time he visited—it was as predictable as an Abbott and Costello conversation about baseball. "You sure? No mochaccino? No double-tall, half-decaf, two-percent with a shot of caramel? I've got some nice mint-flavored cream I could use to make you a breve…"

"Coffee. Black."

"Aw, come on. Just a little fluffy milk? I know how to make a heart on top with the foam."

Patricio made a noise that sounded like a strangled "urrrgh."

She gave an exaggerated sigh, filled the filter with ground Bolivian blend, and flipped the switch. A few seconds later, the save-the-trees mug was full, so she handed it to her brother. "There you go. Coffee. Black. You are so boring."

He took it, then reached out with his free hand to ruffle her hair. "Thanks."

"Don't mention it." After she made herself a quick cappuccino, she got a package of orange-cranberry muffins out of the fridge and took it and her mug over to the table. Patricio grabbed a couple of plates out of the cupboard and followed.

"So what are you doing here?" Sabrina asked as they sat. "I wasn't expecting you, and unfortunately, I'll have to go to work soon." Her house sat on the southern edge of Port Renegade, so it had an unobstructed view of the mountains from the kitchen and dining room. She scanned the ridge as she sipped her coffee, knowing that it wouldn't yield any clues about Tara's disappearance from this distance.

"Handling security for a political fund-raiser," he replied. "Jessie told me about Tara when I called you last night. Said you were down with a migraine and she was here taking care of you, so I came over and sent her home." Wrapping his big hands around the mug, Patricio looked at her… no, *through* her would have been a more appropriate way to phrase it. Of all of her brothers, he seemed to be the one who read her best, who could understand her even when she hadn't said a word.

Still looking out the window, Sabrina pondered the mountain.

"So what's up with this Donovan dude?"

Whipping her head around, Sabrina could only stare at her brother. He took a drink of his coffee, considering her serenely over the mug.

"He was hanging around the house when I got here, but Jessie wouldn't let him in," he continued. "I'm thinking anger issues."

She shrugged, trying to look nonchalant.

"Do I need to make him go away?"

The piece of muffin between her fingers crumbled at the sudden pressure of her hand, raining crumbs down on the tabletop. "What? No!" Patricio was a well-known bodyguard with training in a million different ways to "make someone go away." And as uncomfortable as Aaron now made her, she hardly wanted to sic her mad, bad and dangerous-to-know brother on him.

Then again, with Aaron's cop training and all that muscle, maybe he'd be the one to give Patricio a run for his money.

Something on her face as she contemplated Aaron's muscles must've tipped her brother off, because he set down his coffee cup and leaned forward.

"Are you involved with him?"

Whoa. Now there was an awkward question. Wrapping her hands around her own mug, trying to leach some of the warmth from it, Sabrina dropped her gaze to the maple tabletop and shook her head. "No."

"Sabrina Inez."

Might as well confess. Patricio and his weird intuition would figure it out anyway, damn him to everlasting torment. "We've known each other for a while. We flirted, but..." She paused, thinking about the time she'd run into Aaron at the annual Police Ball. She'd been someone else's date, but they'd danced, they'd talked and they'd danced again. Then she'd said good-night to her date, and she and Aaron had gone to an all-night café, where they'd had coffee and had talked some more, until the sun had risen over the snow-capped Olympic Mountains and the waitress had offered them breakfast. She'd thought about him nonstop for the next few days, thrilled at the sound of his voice when he called her and told her how he was trying to get away to see her again. Before that had happened, his daughter had gone missing. But she didn't want to share all of those details, not even with her brother.

"I think he almost asked me out once, but that's it." Basically, that was all the details boiled down to.

"You were interested in him," Patricio said, not a shred of doubt in his voice at the idea.

"Yes. But..." She bit her lower lip, considering her words. "He's Rosie's father," she told him quietly.

Patricio leaned back in his chair with a low whistle. He knew all about Rosie—she'd spilled her guts to all three of her brothers after declaring Rosie's trail cold. "And you called off the search for his daughter. They never found her, did they?"

Sabrina shook her head, wincing a little at her brother's choice of pronoun. She was the "they" who had never found Rosie Donovan. She was the one who'd had to give up, who'd convinced the entire SAR network and the police it was time to declare the trail cold. How painful that must be to a parent, to have someone get in their face and deliberately kill any last bit of hope they were clinging to. She knew Aaron hated her now, and she had never blamed him for that.

Patricio tapped his fingers against the smooth, green ceramic of his mug, looking as if he was weighing his words as he stared out the window at the mountains. "There are similarities between Tara's disappearance and Rosie's," he said. "But you already knew that."

She nodded, unable to form words around the lump in her throat.

"Before he left last night, Donovan said the police are considering the possibility that you have a serial kidnapper at large. He seemed pretty sure of it, himself."

She knew that, too, but to have it put into words was just too much. Abruptly, she pushed her chair back from the table, leaving her coffee cup full and her muffin barely touched. "I have to shower." *I need a minute.*

Patricio just nodded, a movement which she barely processed before whirling around and heading up the stairs to the master bath. Kicking the door closed once she reached it, she stripped off her sweatpants and fitted T-shirt and turned on the water, closing her eyes with relief as it pounded the skin of her back with its warmth. Steam rose in thin curls around her, and she leaned back and let the water stream over her hair, the sound of the shower jets drowning out everything else.

A serial kidnapper. She could barely bring herself to consider the possibility, although of course it had been lurking in the back of her mind like a malignant shadow.

Rosie Donovan had vanished over six months ago. Which meant that the serial kidnapper was most likely a serial *killer*— Patricio just hadn't wanted to voice that possibility. And if they had a serial killer on their hands...

Tara was already gone.

One more colossal failure to add to a growing list. One more search she'd have to call off when the trail went cold. One more set of parents whose hearts she'd have to break. One more young girl sacrificed to the whims of a madman.

"Dammit, dammit, dammit." She reached her hands up to tangle her fingers in the thick, wet ropes of her hair. And then her hands moved around to her face, scrubbing at her eyes, blending the tears into the water running down her cheeks.

She'd never forget the day Aaron Donovan had started hating her.

"Aaron, it's been two weeks, with no new sign of Rosie."

She mouthed the words in the shower as every last detail of that horrible day came back to her, playing in her mind like a motion picture she couldn't turn off.

She remembered how his mouth had twitched ever so slightly when she'd said his daughter's name. She'd reached up to wipe the rain out of her eyes. She hadn't had time to put on a hat or rain hood, and her hair had been soaked through with icy water just like his. "I'm sorry. I'm so sorry, but you know the likelihood of her surviving up there isn't…" Sabrina hadn't been able to bring herself to even finish that sentence.

His jaw, dusted with more than a five o'clock shadow, clenched tightly, and he quickly turned his head away from her— but not before she saw his gray eyes go wild with an angry grief.

"Aaron, I—" She took a deep, shaky breath. She didn't know what to do with her hands. "I can't even imagine what you're going through. But I had two hikers go missing a few hours ago." Sabrina stopped talking for a moment. Just to gain control, to soften her voice and the words she was about to speak. "They deserve to have us put every last resource we have into finding them." *They still have time*.

He turned back to face her, and Sabrina knew she'd never forget the deep, deep emptiness, the hopelessness in his expression. Every time she'd see him from this moment, it would bring back her failure. Failure to mobilize quickly enough, to get on the ridge fast enough, to find his beautiful teenage daughter before she'd gone so deep into the mountains, she might never be found. Sabrina had been a search-and-rescue tracker for almost ten years now, and it was always painful to tell the families that her team had been too late, that their loved one had stepped off an incline or succumbed to the elements, had encountered a cottonmouth or had fallen into one of the swirling mountain rivers. But she'd never, ever had someone vanish as completely as Rosie Donovan had. Never had to call off a search before she could bring closure to a family.

She'd heard about them, the ones who seemed to vanish. Other trackers had told her their own painful stories. But she'd prayed that such a thing would never occur under her watch. And it hadn't, until Rosie had decided to go hiking alone.

The fifteen-year-old had made it to an old logging road, that much she knew. But the road was still well-traveled by cars, and Rosie's footprints, as well as those of the unknown man who'd been following her had been obscured by tire marks. Sabrina had personally searched that road until the command center had ordered her to stop.

They hadn't found a single trace of Rosie Donovan, or her probable assailant.

Vanished.

"My daughter is still alive," Aaron ground out, and though his words were spoken softly, each one had the weight of stone. "I know this."

Sabrina couldn't bring herself to respond.

A slight movement drew her glance downward. Aaron's hands were clenched into white-knuckled fists, but that didn't stop her from seeing that he was trying to keep them from shaking. Heaven help her, Aaron Donovan, one of the Port Renegade Police Department's best detectives, was about to fall apart, and she was the reason. Her failure. Her decision. "She's been with me all her life," he continued, oblivious to Sabrina's thoughts. "I'd know it if she were gone." It was a statement, not a question, thank God. She couldn't have answered it if it had been.

"I wish—" Sabrina stopped. She couldn't leave him room to argue with her, to persuade her to keep throwing valuable time and resources at a hopeless cause. She tried to soften her words by putting a hand on his arm. He didn't even seem to feel her touch. She could practically feel him willing her to say that word, to ignore the missing hikers from Tacoma and keep the search going, to go up on the ridge one more time and bring back his daughter. "We can't keep searching forever, Aaron," she said.

The look he gave her then made her ache. "I can."

With a quick, jerky movement, Sabrina twisted the shower knob, abruptly stopping the water and the memory along with it. God, it hurt to think about Rosie, about Aaron. It hurt to think about what had happened to Tara.

Yanking open the shower curtain with a jerk that caused the metal holders to scream against the shower bar in protest, Sabrina stepped out, wrapping a towel around her body. It had been less than twenty-four hours. They could still find Tara. No matter what had happened to Rosie, Tara still had a chance, and Sabrina would give everything she had to try to bring Tara home. Safe. Alive. And if she happened to find the person who'd stolen Tara away in the process, she'd tear him apart.

Sabrina quickly dressed for work in a

long-sleeved blue T-shirt, thick socks and a pair of nylon twill hiking pants lined with moisture-wicking mesh—not the sexiest things she owned, but they would keep her warm on the ridge. Pulling her towel-dried hair back into a messy knot on top of her head, she padded back downstairs to the kitchen, where her brother was still waiting for her.

"So, about Donovan..." he began without preamble, leaning against the kitchen island. "I think you should be careful. Word on the street is even though he's returned to work and is trying to be a functioning member of society, he's still pretty messed up."

The implication behind his words made her forget all about the probably lukewarm coffee she'd been about to grab off the table. "Word on the—? How would you know what the word on the street in Port Renegade is? You just got here."

He flashed a grin at her. "Made some calls." As usual, he didn't volunteer any more information. All the better to look like Creepily All-Seeing Big Brother, ready to jump out and smother you with overprotectiveness at the least sign of something suspicious.

"At six-twenty in the morning you made some calls? Who is up at oh-dark-hundred waiting to spill all the secrets of our fair city?"

"If I told you that, I'd have to—"

She rolled her eyes. "Kill me?"

"Nah. Just make you my receptionist."

Sabrina grunted, taking a sip of the now lukewarm brew. It'd be a cold day in you-know-where before she'd confine herself to an office job, even at her beloved brother's security company. "He's a good cop, Rico. He got an award from the city last year for having an amazing homicide solve rate—I think the paper said somewhere over ninety percent."

"Makes sense. My contact said the chief of police was willing to do backflips to keep him on board." Patricio leaned back against the table, bracing himself with his hands. "All Donovan's doing at work right now is reporting in once a week to shuffle some papers around so the brass can feel like they're keeping an eye on him. Spends most of his time in the park."

Clutching the mug with both hands, Sabrina looked down, tracing the patterns on her hardwood floor with her eyes. "Searching for his daughter," she said quietly. Rosie had been hiking the Dungeness River Trail the last time anyone had seen her. The trail made a figure eight to the Dungeness River Falls and back, and she saw the smooth-soled prints of shiny black cop shoes every time she herself stepped on it. She'd stopped going to the Falls after a while.

Patricio stepped forward and took the mug from her, placing it on the counter behind her. Then, he cupped her arms with his hands. "Look, I know you feel you owe the guy something, but the fact is, he's a little unhinged. Understandably so, but that doesn't mean you shouldn't be careful."

Sabrina patted his knuckles, trying to make the gesture as reassuring as possible. "I will, big brother. Don't worry."

"You sure you don't need me to talk to the guy? I'd feel a lot better."

"I'd *really* rather you didn't." She shook her head, unable to help but smile a little at the thought of her big, scary brother having a word with the big, scary police detective. "I can handle him."

"Well." Patricio blew his slightly too-long bangs off his forehead, obviously not crazy about her answer but respecting it all the same. "In that case, go get some practice. He's standing outside your door."

AARON DONOVAN felt like a ghost.

For the past six months, he had pulled it together enough to go through the motions of his life—eating when he remembered, getting up, going to work, talking to people when he had to, coming home again, going outside for a run when the silence in the house became too much for him. But during all of it, he felt like a dispassionate observer, floating above his body and watching it interact, function, stay employed. Stay alive.

He lifted his hand to knock on Sabrina's door, and was almost surprised that he couldn't see the brightly painted wood right through his fingers. Every day, a little more of him felt as though it had disappeared.

The only thing keeping him from floating away entirely was the hope—no, the knowledge that Rosie was still alive, that somewhere, she still needed him. And so, every day, he climbed up the ridge and walked along the paths, not bothering to talk to anyone, hardly seeing his surroundings. His sole focus was finding his daughter again.

He let his hand fall, and in a well-practiced movement, took his wallet out of his jacket pocket and flipped to the worn photo in its plastic sleeve. Rosie had his grandmother's smile—a huge, toothy grin that could light up a room. Her reddish-brown curls bounced all over her head, as if even her hair responded to her vivacious personality. She loved obese cats, cherry taffy from the county fair, and horrible teenage prime-time soap operas that she'd always made him watch with her, bribing him with giant bowls of popcorn and his favorite root beer. She was larger than life, his girl. She was the sweetest person he'd ever known.

She was gone.

The hardest thing about knowing Rosie was still alive was also knowing that she was a victim, every hour, every day that went past. He didn't know who had her. He didn't know what that person was doing to her. He didn't know if she'd ever be even close to the same when she came back.

And worst of all, he couldn't hold her, and fix the problem just as he had so many little-girl problems throughout their life together. This was no little-girl problem.

But what he did not doubt was that she was still alive. If she really had been gone, he would have felt it, wouldn't be propelled out of bed every morning and pushed into going on if her presence hadn't been there to guide him. His cop sense couldn't fail him now, not about something so important. And so he haunted the mountains, like a specter on the trails, refusing to give up the search even after everyone else he'd counted on had left him alone.

The huge, black hulking *thing* that followed him everywhere, waiting for him to show just a moment of weakness so it could swallow him whole, moved closer— despair waiting to choke the life out of him. So he snapped his wallet closed, cut off the brutal memories without a moment's regret, and detached, floated away from the visions of his daughter. He had a job to do.

He reached up again and knocked on Sabrina's door.

"Did you mean to take down the whole door? Because there's a bell." The door swung inward as her voice preceded her outside. Then, her face followed—whiskey-colored eyes, tan skin over angular cheekbones and a square jaw. Her straight black hair was pulled up, as usual. Besides yesterday on the trails, he'd only seen it fall to her shoulders once, when he'd asked her to let it down.

A lifetime ago, he'd thought her beautiful. She probably still was, but it didn't matter now.

Sabrina's hand tightened on the door as soon as she saw him. Offering him a tentative, "Hello, Aaron," she kept the heavy wood pivoted slightly between her body and his, as if he were some kind of threat. Part of him hated himself for scaring her, and part of him was glad he could.

Her eyes, the color of aged Scotch, changed as she looked at him, going from wary to concerned. And maybe it was the fact that he'd been out all night and hadn't changed out of his rumpled, muddy suit.

Maybe it was the way the past twenty-four hours had been a perverse replay of the day his daughter had disappeared. But it was the concern that brought him back into his body, made him feel an echo of something he'd thought long gone. Even though he probably looked like a madman to her, she looked like refuge to him. All he wanted to do was sink into her, inhale the fresh scent of her hair that he remembered so well, and forget about everything.

Dammit, she was still beautiful.

"Aaron? Did you want something, or are you just going to hover?" Her words held a tinge of sarcasm, but her white-knuckled hands still clutching the door told another story. She may have been concerned, but she was still afraid.

"Aaron?" she repeated.

Aaron? We're out of leads. I'm sorry. I'm so sorry.

Right. Sorry, but not willing to do anything about it.

"Can I come in?" he finally said to Sabrina, his voice sounding raw even to his ears, as though someone had run sandpaper across his vocal cords. "I have news."

He heard her gasp as she stepped back

and swung the door open, and he moved inside before she could change her mind. Her house was small, but it had a cozy feel to it—as if she'd intentionally chosen a smaller, low-maintenance place rather than spreading out in one of the newer tract mansions that were rising daily on the side of the city along the shores of the Hood Canal. It didn't have the damp reek of poverty and despair he'd found in other small houses, on other work-related calls.

"Coffee, Detective?"

He turned around, surprised to hear her address him that way. She'd always called him Aaron. Even when he'd started spitting her last name back at her, a sarcastic "Ms." carelessly tacked on. Clearly, she was trying to put some verbal distance between them, because there sure as hell wasn't much space in the tiny room. A puffy, deep red couch was pushed up against one wall, the rest of the room taken up by a matching chair and ottoman, an old trunk used as a coffee table, and more throw pillows than he figured were necessary.

He shook his head. "No, thanks." He let his hand trail across the embroidered quilt she'd slung over the sofa, listening to the sounds of the old house around them. "Someone else is here."

"My brother." She sank down on the edge the chair, tucking her feet behind the ottoman, hands holding her knees. "He's showering. You said you had news?" She gestured to the sofa in silent invitation, and he sat down.

Not knowing what else to do, he dove right in. "Does Tara Fisher's disappearance feel at all similar to you, to when...?" He stopped, unable to put the event into words, unable to compromise his carefully put-together facade.

"To when Rosie disappeared?" she finished softly. "You know it does, Aaron. Otherwise, why did you take the call yesterday on the ridge? I know missing persons isn't your territory." She grabbed an orange pillow off the couch and hugged it to her chest like a barrier.

He leaned forward, elbows on his knees, doing his best to look like a professional cop and not some poor bastard who was about to fall apart. "We don't have conclusive evidence, but we're considering the possibility that we have a serial kidnapper on the loose. Too many coincidences."

She regarded him thoughtfully for a moment, her slender fingers digging into the pillow's softness. She didn't try changing the word *kidnapper* to *killer,* which made him breathe easier for a moment. "Two girls around the same age," she said thoughtfully, "disappearing from under the park rangers' noses with no real clues left behind."

He nodded.

"So why are you here, then?"

"Sabrina, the cop who took the call when Tara went missing is still new to the force. He didn't even realize that he could call in the park search and rescue."

"What about his partner? Surely the department doesn't put two rookies together."

"Eddie Ventaglia is working with him now. He's Rosie's godfather." He knew she'd put two and two together, so he wouldn't have to explain that Eddie thought SAR had botched the search for Rosie and made calling them in again his last resort. It had happened before, ever since Aaron's daughter had vanished. "The only reason you got called at all was because I intervened, once I came in and found out what was going on."

She seemed taken aback by that. "Why? I mean, why did you bring us in?"

He picked a pen up off the coffee table, flipping it back and forth between his fingers. "Because I know you're the best in the state. And I knew you were our best chance of finding out what's happened to Tara." He stopped flipping the pen and looked directly into her eyes. "Regardless of what happened...before."

"Uh, thanks." She blinked at him a few times. "Aaron, I have no idea where this is going, but I'm dying to understand. Because I know you'd have to want something to be here."

"I don't have Chief Webber's blessing to act until we have more conclusive evidence." He practically spat out the last three words, because what they really meant was that the police wouldn't throw every resource they had into finding the man until another girl went missing. "I'm talking to Skylar about putting a security escort on your teams." He steeled himself for what he knew wasn't going to be a shiny, happy reaction.

He was right. "What?" Her head snapped up, and she tossed the pillow she'd been holding to the side with disgusted force. "You've got to be kidding me. You guys muck up our scenes well enough without my team having its own personal Godzilla stomping all over the tracks we're trying to follow."

"It doesn't work that way, and you know it." The local and state police departments had often called in park search and rescue to assist with tracking fugitives and the like. The more dangerous the criminal they'd been trying to apprehend, the more police protection went on the trail with the trackers. Generally, the cops brought up the rear, keeping their eyes out for danger from ahead and above, and letting tracking groups of two or three comb the ground before them. It wasn't ideal in terms of protection, but it was the only way to let the trackers do their job without the cops, as she'd put it, mucking up the trail.

She leaned forward, her eyes practically giving off sparks. "Not calling us for two hours when someone goes missing in the park doesn't work that way, either, but you know those rookies," she snapped. "We don't need babysitters."

The same frustration he'd felt when the

police chief had told him in no uncertain terms that he wasn't assuming they had a serial kidnapper on their hands unless a third person went missing, under the same circumstances, bubbled up inside him. It was his daughter, dammit, and this was the first break they'd had. There was no way he was going to sit passively on the sidelines while everyone around him went to work, no way he'd put Rosie's life solely in someone else's hands. If Sabrina went on that mountain looking for their guy, he'd be there, too.

"I'm not suggesting you get a rookie on your team," he said. "I meant me."

"You?" She blinked, confusion, denial and apprehension all apparent in the look she gave him. And then she shook her head. "No. Oh, no. Not you."

That irritated him. He was a homicide detective with over fifteen years of experience, as well as a former marine sniper and a veteran of the Panama Invasion and the first Gulf War. On paper, he would have looked damned attractive to any tracking team working in an area with a violent criminal lurking around. But he knew it was his behavior after losing Rosie that caused her reaction. Intellectually, he knew the fact that his daughter hadn't been found wasn't Sabrina's fault. But the day she'd told him she was calling off the search still ranked among the most painful of his life, and he still felt it.

But for Rosie, he had to push that all aside. So he tried a different tactic, a more reasonable tactic, hoping for a peaceful resolution to their current standoff. "I'll stay in the background. You know I won't compromise the trails."

"Jessie told me you've been on leave for the past six months, Aaron, and you only came back to work a week ago. Part-time."

Translation: *You're too much of a head case over your daughter's disappearance to be of any help to us.*

He took a deep breath, refusing to let her get to him. "You and Jessie aren't much older than Tara Fisher. We've worked together before—you know I'd be good to have around if there's someone dangerous in those woods. And I can't—" He broke off before she could hear the tremor in his voice, the one that was working its way through his entire body. *Control, Donovan. Keep it together. Just for a few more minutes.* "I can't just *sit* here. This is the first solid lead we've had in months." Even if Webber didn't see it that way.

Whether it was the something close to naked pleading in his voice or the fact that she knew he wouldn't back down, at that moment he knew he had her. Sabrina's shoulders slumped and she closed her eyes, the fight in her leaking out like air from a punctured balloon. And even though it wasn't like him—or the him he'd been months ago—he used what he could to exploit her moment of weakness, because he had to.

"You owe me, Sabrina."

She looked down at her hands. A worry line appeared between her dark eyebrows, and he could practically see her grinding her teeth in frustration. But she didn't respond, and he knew her silence meant she wouldn't say no to him—not now, not ever. Not when he had struck that low a blow.

He looked down at the top of her head, her hair shiny from the thin, cloud-filtered sunlight that came through the sheer curtains on the living-room window. And then, because he couldn't think of anything else to say, he walked out. Leaving didn't make him feel any better about himself.

Chapter Four

Sabrina pulled her Jeep out of her driveway just as the first of the morning light slipped over the horizon, painting the place where the sky met the mountains a dark shade of magenta. Thank God she was in motion again, doing something with the excess energy that had had her punching her pillow and staring at the ceiling all night.

Unfortunately, sitting in her car while she drove with only the hum of the engine to keep her company did absolutely nothing to quiet her thoughts, which had insisted on racing between the two missing girls ever since yesterday afternoon. *Rosie, Tara, Rosie, Tara, Rosie, Tara*—a demented mantra that just might drive her insane if she didn't get on that mountain and get working soon. Breathe in: *Rosie*. Breathe out: *Tara*. She could only hope that hitting the trails would give her some peace.

Then again, Aaron hadn't had anything remotely resembling a peaceful moment for six months. What made her think she deserved that?

Reaching over to snap on the radio, she glanced up as a pair of headlights flashed in her rearview mirror. As Shawn Colvin's clear voice rang out into the quiet, she wasn't at all surprised to see a boxy sedan pull away from the curb about half a block behind her. A few minutes later, when she turned onto the county road that would take her to the gates of Renegade Ridge State Park, the other car did the same, always keeping a respectable distance from her back bumper.

"Well, good morning, Detective Donovan," she murmured to the headlights. "I was wondering where you'd gone."

She hadn't given him an answer to his "request" to join her tracking team earlier that morning. But they both knew when he walked out her front door that she was going to cave and let him. Guilt was a funny thing. She'd thought he would just head for the ranger station without her, but apparently he preferred to follow her. In a mysterious and creepy way.

"All the better to intimidate the stuffing out of you, my dear," she muttered under her breath, disgusted with herself for letting Aaron—no, not Aaron, his *car*—get under her skin. Slapping down the turn signal, she steered her car left onto Mountain View Drive, which would lead her to the main park entrance. Aaron, of course, followed.

She could think of a million reasons why she should tell him to take a flying leap off her tracking team's universe—he was distracting and an inexperienced tracker. He was a very angry human time bomb, and seeing as she was indirectly the cause of his anger…things could get ugly indeed if they hung around together for extended periods of time.

Most of all, being around him was just too hard. She missed him as he'd been… before. He'd never been much of a talker, but he'd had an easy way about him. He'd actually listened to people, focusing those calm, gorgeous eyes on you with his entire being, as if he could see down to your bones. No judgment, no ulterior motive. Just the oh-so-sexy feeling that the things you thought about and cared for were important to him. And when she'd finally gotten him to open up, using every ounce of charm she possessed with a good dose of nonstop chatter in between, it had been amazing. He was intelligent. He made her laugh. He had an innate sense of, not to sound corny, but…honor that was apparent in everything he said or did. When he'd told her that he joined the police force because he wanted "to serve and protect, just like the badge says," she believed in him. One hundred percent.

Brushing a stray strand of hair out of her eyes, she glanced in the mirror again. "I miss you," she told the headlights dancing behind her in the dimly lit morning. But then she jerked her gaze back to the road, pushing the sudden ache she felt out of her mind with sheer force of will. That Aaron, the one she missed, was gone, leaving behind just the ghost of a man, understandably wrapped up in grief and bitterness. Nothing she could do would bring him back, short of finding his poor, poor daughter.

And what were the chances of that?

Sabrina slowed the Jeep down as the park

gates came into view. The sun had finally cleared the mountainous horizon, though the light was, of course, filtered through a thick, unbroken blanket of clouds that stretched in every direction.

She flashed her park badge at the ranger at the admission booth and kept driving. Since he wasn't a park employee, Aaron had to stop and pay the service fee, but he soon caught up to her, following her to the ranger station. Inside, Skylar would brief and dispatch the teams. Sabrina figured the site coordinator would most likely center the search around the logging road on which Tara Fisher's trail had abruptly ended in the hopes that one of them would pick it up again.

She immediately quashed the impulse to calculate the odds of that.

She parked her Jeep in the lot outside the ranger station, a large building constructed out of pine logs in the style of a Northwest hunting lodge, out of stripped pine logs, complete with a wraparound porch lined with weathered Adirondack chairs for visitors to sit in and admire the view of the mountains. By the time she stepped out of her vehicle, Aaron was already standing by its door, waiting.

The gigantic rifle he held in both hands caught her eye first, its muzzle pointing toward the sky. The weapon boasted a large scope attachment and a thick canvas carrying strap with sturdy buckles to snap it in place. Aaron himself was all in black so the rifle blended in with his body— black T-shirt and black cargo pants tucked into a pair of military-issue black boots.

"Hunting elephants today, Detective?" It was a lame joke, but it popped out before she could stop herself. Leaving her pack and walking stick in the car, she smacked a palm against the door to close it, keeping a wary eye on his gun. She sure wouldn't want to slog up the trails with that thing, unless she could use it as a walking stick.

Aaron didn't respond. He just focused his deep-set gray eyes on her, and she shivered at the hollowness in them, knowing without a doubt that the man before her was capable of using the gun he held. Patricio was right—he did seem a little unhinged, today more so than usual. She half expected him to swing the rifle around and pump a shell into place like a Hollywood action hero, just to try to scare her. Then again, the rifle didn't appear to have a pump action. At least, not like the ones she'd seen in movies. She knew zero about guns, other than that she didn't like them.

Seemingly unperturbed by her scrutiny, Aaron quietly hooked his right arm through the carrying strap and brought the strap over his head, so the rifle ended up resting comfortably across his back, the muzzle pointing barrel down. The olive-green nylon pulled tight against his chest, curving over his pecs and hugging his flat abs over his T-shirt.

She swallowed, indicating the weapon with a wave of her hand. "Do you really think you'll need that?"

"I told you I'd protect you. And your team." He brought an arm across his chest and touched his hand against the rifle stock. The gesture seemed casual, but somehow she knew he could and would pull that scary-looking gun up into place in seconds. "I take my promises seriously."

Unlike you. He might as well have said the words, because they were hanging in the air between them all the same. She turned her body away from him slightly, so he couldn't see how much his attitude bothered her, wishing that she'd had the guts to stop second-guessing herself and tell Aaron exactly what he could do with his big gun.

Then again, part of her was actually glad for the firepower. She'd always felt more than safe with Alex and Jessie at her side, but now, the things Aaron had put into words brought home that something was in these woods that called for deadly force. Without him, her team would simply be very exposed, and very alone.

At the sound of footsteps, she looked up to see Alex jogging toward them. Several yards behind him, Jessie turned her small blue pickup into the parking lot.

"Whoa, what's up with G.I. Donovan here?" Alex directed his question at Sabrina, then without waiting for an answer, pulled on the gray Evergreen University sweatshirt he'd been carrying to ward off the morning chill. "He pulling security detail on our team?"

Both men looked at her. Good question. Was he? *Yes or no, Adelante.*

She took a deep breath, then nodded.

Aaron's expression didn't change, but she noticed the smallest bit of tension leave his shoulders at her confirmation that he would be joining them.

Alex stepped pretty much right into Aaron's personal space, looking him up and down. "Skylar okay with this? I don't see any other cops here this morning." Several more cars were pulling up behind the spot where Jessie had parked her truck, and small groups of people in conversation had sprung up around the parking lot. Alex was right—the faces around them were all familiar members of Port Renegade SAR, without police security escorts.

"Yes, Skylar okayed it, and I'm not a cop today," Aaron said. "Just an everyday citizen volunteering to help his local search-and-rescue squad."

"In that case, dude—" Alex made a big show of circling Aaron to check out the rifle slung across his back. "We're tracking a teenager, not infiltrating terrorist cells."

Aaron quirked a corner of his mouth upward, Alex's challenge putting an interesting gleam in his eye. He didn't respond to the taunt, but he did start turning slowly to match Alex's movements. Kind of like a cobra watching a snake charmer. Except Alex wasn't exactly being charming.

At that moment, Jessie walked up to stand beside Sabrina, her pale, freckled complexion looking pink and freshly scrubbed. "What's up with those two?" The blonde planted her walking stick into the ground and leaned on it, narrowing her eyes at the two men.

Sabrina made a small gesture with her chin toward Aaron. "Big gun." She cocked her head in Alex's direction. "Naked male insecurity."

"Hey!" Alex swung his head around to confront them. "I just want to make sure Detective Donovan isn't going to trip on his big gun and shoot himself in the ass, is all. Or worse, shoot one of us, since we'll be walking in front of him."

Aaron didn't say anything, though the sound he made signified that he clearly found the statement ridiculous.

"Al, you're being a child." With that dismissive comment, Jessie crouched down to tighten the laces on her hiking boots.

"No, really." His posture had gone all

bar-brawl, chest out, arms swinging with frustrated challenge. "If the good detective here thinks he can do our job better than we can, why can't I carry the big gun, then?"

Aaron scrubbed a hand across his face, obviously tiring of the conversation. "Again, I'm volunteering," he said with calm, measured patience.

"Can we un-volunteer you?"

"Ask your team leader."

Alex glanced at Sabrina, and she knew that part of this show was for her benefit. She and Alex had been friends and then colleagues since the beginning of time, and he well knew that being close to Aaron would upset her, at best. She stepped forward, put her hand on Alex's arm. "It's okay. I asked him to come."

Aaron blinked, obviously startled at her stretching of the truth. Sure, he'd had to play the guilt card to get her to let him join them, but now that she'd accepted his presence, she might as well try to make peace between all of them. As much as she could, anyway.

"You sure?" Alex asked softly.

She nodded.

He turned back to Aaron, running a hand

through his close-cropped black hair—his "good luck" Mariners cap presumably still in his car. "All right. But I really do want to know how qualified you are with that gun. Because last I'd heard, you weren't SWAT and you don't carry Remington M-24s around every day on the job."

Shifting his weight from foot to foot, Aaron weighed his response for a moment. "I'm a U.S. Marine."

"My old man was a marine. He was also a drunk."

Inhaling deeply through his nose, Aaron rolled his eyes, his mouth tightening. "Fine. U.S. Marine Corps sergeant, Third Battalion, Eighth Marine Regiment, graduated from the USMC Scout Sniper School."

Alex folded his arms, narrowing his eyes at the cop. "How'd you graduate?"

"Scout Sniper Qualified."

Alex gave a low whistle. "Okay, he can stay." Most of the groups around them had started heading inside the ranger station, and he moved to join them. Apparently, whatever Aaron had said had satisfied him. Now if only Sabrina had an idea of what it all meant, including Alex's abrupt change of heart—though she guessed the word *sniper* was a giant clue.

"What?" Jessie bolted forward to catch up with Alex, tugging on the sleeve of his windbreaker and bringing him to a stop. "What does that mean? What?"

He let her turn him back toward their group, looking at Aaron with more approval than challenge this time. "It means that Donovan here is among the top one percent in the world."

"At sniping people?" Jessie asked.

"Exactly."

"Huh." Dropping her hand from Alex's sleeve, Jessie gave Aaron a small smile. "Thanks for coming with us. Your being a police detective was good enough for me, so I'm sorry Alex gave you such a hard time." She and Alex made their way to the station's glass double doors, still bickering companionably. Jessie had gotten divorced about a year earlier, a few months before she'd joined Sabrina's team. She rarely talked about her ex-husband, but Sabrina had gotten the idea that she wasn't pining away for the man. She sometimes hoped Jessie and Alex might hit it off, but they acted more like brother and sister, with a dash of Alex's obnoxious flirting thrown in.

Whatever the case, the important thing was that they'd both apparently accepted Aaron's presence on the team, so all they had left to do was get their assignments from Skylar and get to work. Maybe today they'd get lucky and find some glaring clue that would lead them straight to Tara. Maybe...

She glanced at Aaron.

Don't think.

As if he somehow knew where her mind had just gone, Aaron flicked his eyes at her, the small bit of amusement that had been in them a few moments earlier long gone.

"I don't—" she began, then stopped. "I'm glad you're here, too." Now that she'd had time to push her gut reaction aside and really think about the new danger in the woods, she was. "Thank you."

He was so still, so silent, he looked as if he'd frozen in place. And again, he stole her breath. She was aware of every sound—the voices around them, the morning breeze whistling through the evergreens towering above, the snick of someone closing a car door, the shrill cry of a blackbird circling through the clouds, her own heartbeat.

"Don't thank me. I'm not here for you."

She closed her eyes, heard Aaron walk away, far from her, leaving her with only her guilt, a heavy weight pressing hard inside her chest.

SKYLAR SENT Sabrina's team back where they'd been yesterday, to the location where Tara's trail had ended, telling them to cut for sign along the sides of the old logging road to see if they could pick it back up. She dispatched the other teams strategically up and down the road and throughout the park, miles apart, creating a net of searchers that they hoped would converge on Tara's trail, once it reappeared.

Unfortunately, the more time went by, the less likely that seemed.

The four of them slogged through the snarling undergrowth along the sides of the gravel road and fanned down through the trees all morning and afternoon, scouring the roadsides for telltale broken plants, snapped twigs, and even partial prints that would tell them Tara's trail continued. But the few leads they'd thought they found always turned out to be paths made by animals. No one had walked along this roadside in a long time, except for the original set of tracks they'd followed down the ridge the day before. All signs pointed to Tara being taken off the mountain by car. But because it was their job, they continued the search, hoping that something would catch their eye and the hunt would be on again. Throughout it all, Aaron followed several feet behind the three of them, silent and so stealthy, they couldn't hear him at all and only knew he was there when they turned to check. He hadn't said much to them at all, even when they'd stopped, but she knew he had to be getting impatient with their lack of results. Tracking could be maddening even when you were used to it.

Fifteen minutes before total darkness, they were forced to call it a day, with nothing to show for it. They made their way back to Sabrina's Jeep and rode in silence back to the ranger station, defeat practically hanging in the air. Once inside, they sat at one of the tables assembled inside the main room, where the teams would all report to Skylar on what they'd found once everyone was assembled.

Knowing from the day's intermittent radio transmissions that none of the other teams had had any luck, Sabrina knew that Skylar would have the unenviable task of telling the Fishers that their beloved daughter was still missing.

Alex and Jessie sat next to Sabrina at the side of the table where they could face Skylar. Aaron walked around to the other side and pulled up a metal folding chair directly across from Sabrina. She could tell he was in the mood for some kind of conversation, and to be honest, the thought kind of freaked her out a little.

"What now?" he asked, tipping his head toward her and keeping his voice low. And damn if the intimate sound of it didn't send her mind in every direction it shouldn't have gone. She'd always loved his voice, a deep, resonant bass she could have picked out of a crowd of people all speaking at once. Once upon a time, she could have listened to him talk all night long. In fact, she had once. Ages ago.

"We report to Skylar, and we keep going." She hoped her own voice sounded professional, detached, that it didn't give a hint of where her thoughts had strayed.

"I'm sure the admissions people have given any records of the cars that passed through the gates yesterday to the police, but there are hundreds of them every day."

He nodded. "Eddie said they're running the license plates to see if we come up with any stolen cars or known pedophiles as registered owners. We're also trying to get a match on that tire track we cast yesterday to help narrow things down. But the chief isn't ruling out that Tara's not just a lost hiker, so Eddie's the only one working this case right now. Along with about nine other cases."

It was the most he'd said to any of them all day. "At least they're checking the cars." She leaned her forehead against her palm, rubbing her hairline and trying not to give in to her fatigue before the briefing started.

"Ready to give up already?" His words were so soft, she was sure Alex and Jessie had no clue what he'd just said. Which was probably fine with Aaron, as they were without a doubt meant for her.

"That's not fair!" She leaned forward so quickly in her chair, the metal legs shrieked as they scraped against the hardwood floor.

Sabrina tried never to get angry at someone who'd lost a family member in the parklands under her watch, no matter how belligerent they got in their desperation. It all just stemmed from caring so deeply for someone and being too helpless to do anything to bring them home. But she'd been Aaron's whipping girl for far too long. "I had no choice but to call off the search, and you know it. Blame me all you want, but it's not going to change what I did six months ago, and it's not going to make me think I was wrong." *Sure*. "And it's also not going to bring Rosie back."

He reared back as if she'd hit him at the mention of his daughter's name, but then quickly collected himself. "What would you do? If it had been your daughter, or your sister? One of your nieces?"

Her stomach clenched at the mere thought of her adopted sister's beautiful children disappearing under those circumstances. "I'd do exactly what you're doing, Aaron. But I wouldn't blame the searchers for not blowing off everyone else who got lost and needed help."

He stood and swept an arm at the crowd

of trackers that had nearly filled the large room. "Like you don't have enough people here to find all of Seattle if the entire city got lost at the same time."

She stood up with him, feeling suddenly cold. Hell if she'd let him tower over her like that. "You have no idea what you're talking about." She kept her voice low, but her coworkers were still starting to stare, and Alex and Jessie had long since dropped any pretense of not listening in. "I made the right decision."

He braced his hands on the table and leaned toward her. "You gave up."

Her vision blurred for a moment, whether from anger or tears, she didn't care. "That, Aaron Donovan, is a lie," she said quietly. Reaching into her jacket pocket, Sabrina fumbled for the piece of paper she always carried with her. With shaking hands, she unfolded it, not caring that it was so worn from handling, it might tear. She knew what was on it like she knew her own voice. But still she carried it, hoping that she'd have a chance to compare it to… something. Once the paper was open, she placed it on the table and pushed it toward him.

A footprint. A sketch of one, actually—
a size-seven Timberland women's hiking-
boot print, with a cross-patterned sole, worn
on the inside curve of the heel from the way
its owner had distributed her weight when
she'd walked.

Time seemed to stop for a moment. All
Aaron seemed able to do was stare at the
drawing under her hand. All she could do
was breathe, keep breathing and try her
damnedest not to cry.

He raised his head, and his expression
was softer, more vulnerable than Sabrina
ever remembered seeing him, under-
standing dawning in those unfathomable
gray eyes.

"Rosie's?" he asked gently.

"I never stopped looking for her," she
said, shaking from the effort it took to hold
her emotions in. "Every time I go up on
these trails, I'm always looking for her."
She backed away from the table, needing to
get as far away from him as possible. "And
now, Detective, you can go. Because it'll be
over my dead body that I keep you, and
your accusations and your bitterness on my
team. We worked ourselves into the ground

trying to find Rosie, and not one of us in this room will ever stop. We all deserve better than that."

Chapter Five

Later that evening, when Aaron turned
his car onto the street where his house sat,
he wasn't surprised to see Mary Beth
Peterson's lime-green Beetle parked in his
driveway. Just what he needed, a little
cheer from the home office to cap a truly
crappy day.

After pulling into his driveway next to
the little car, he got a small, perverse
amount of pleasure in taking his sweet time
getting out of the car, checking and double-
checking that his headlights were turned
off, fussing with his keys, shuffling through
some ancient mail that had been moldering
on the passenger seat for about a week. In-
dulging his passive aggression was pretty
much the only way he'd be able to vent his
annoyance at the woman's arrival. There

was just something about her round face and sunshiny demeanor that made it impossible to be overtly rude to her without feeling like the lowest form of pond scum afterward—the kind of jerk who clubbed baby seals in his spare time.

Patience, Donovan. Blowing out a loud whoosh of air, he braced himself for her relentless cheer and opened the door. Once outside, he leaned his arms on the roof of his Crown Vic, allowing her to make the next move. The next happy, happy, singsongy move.

The psychiatrist was perched on the two-seater swing that sat on his wraparound porch, swinging her bare feet in front of her, her lime-green Crocs abandoned near the porch's top step. Her curly gray bob bounced as she tilted her head to get a better look at him. "Hello, Aaron." She smiled, revealing two deep dimples in each chubby cheek. She shifted her rear slightly as if to plant herself more solidly on the swing, a solid nonverbal message that she wasn't going anywhere.

Which put him in a very, very bad mood. Talk was time wasted, and he had very little time to spare.

Smacking his palms lightly against the roof, he pushed off the car and made his way toward the house. "Mary Beth." He nodded at her and pulled his keys out of his pocket. Maybe if he pretended that seeing her on his porch was nothing out of the ordinary, he could sneak inside and ignore her until she went away.

"Come chat with me a minute? It's such a nice night."

He'd just about had the key in the lock, but her request stilled his hand. Some stupid shred of manners his mother had ingrained in him made it impossible to leave Mary Beth alone. He pocketed the keys and moved to the porch railing, leaning back against it and folding his arms.

Her hands tucked under her thighs, Mary Beth kept swinging her bare feet, her expression pleasant and supportive. He wondered if she had learned that in medical school, practicing in front of a mirror until she could freeze her face that way no matter what bat-crap-crazy thing a patient might utter.

As always, Mary Beth broke the silence between them. "Well, Aaron, I was just checking to see how you're doing."

"I'm fine, Mary Beth, thanks for asking." He shifted his weight. "How are you?"

She gave a little half laugh. "I'm great. You always have such nice manners, even when I know I sometimes catch you at a bad time."

"You didn't catch me at a bad time." Liar, liar, liar.

She winked at him, as if to say that she well knew he hated her visits. He wished he could tell her that it was nothing personal. As the floating shrink who served at least three city police departments in Clallam County, Mary Beth had the unenviable job of counseling any and all officers who were dealing with what their supervisors deemed an undue amount of stress. And most cops, by nature, didn't want to admit that they were anything but strong enough to take whatever the job could throw at them, even "events of a traumatic nature," as she liked to put it.

Such a clinical phrase. *Events of a traumatic nature*. A clean, sterile way to describe having his heart ripped out of his chest when his daughter was taken.

He wished she and Chief Webber would just accept that trying to counsel him was useless. You couldn't just put a Band-Aid over the gaping hole in his life Rosie had left behind and pretend everything was all better. He'd gone back to work on a very part-time basis just to get both of them off his back, but he probably hadn't fooled anyone. He was just going through the motions, a ghost doomed to meaningless, repetitive action until he found his little girl again.

His teeth clenched together so tightly, he felt the pain radiate through his jaw. He would find her. Because the alternative was unthinkable.

Mary Beth broke into his thoughts, chatting about the pleasant weather they'd had last week and the new cooking class she'd been taking. And then, after a few more minutes of small talk, she zoomed in on her real purpose for coming.

"So I hear you went back on leave," she said. "How is that working out?"

"It's working out fine."

She nodded, folding her hands in her lap, still swinging slowly back and forth, pushing off with her bare toes. "I heard about Tara Fisher. You're helping to look for her?"

It didn't surprise him that she'd figured out what he'd chosen to do with his time, even though he'd told no one at the precinct. He nodded curtly.

"I hope you find her. I can only imagine how her family must feel."

Yeah, well, he knew exactly how they felt, how they were going to feel if Tara never came home. "The chief doesn't think they're connected." Dammit, he hadn't meant to blurt that out, but there it was. Sometimes, he thought Mary Beth was too talented a listener for her own good. "I couldn't take the chance that they weren't."

She planted her feet on the ground, stopping the swing's lazy motion. "I understand." And he knew she had, following his train of thought to the connection between Rosie's and Tara's disappearances without him having to say the words. "You do what you have to do. I'm sure the Fishers appreciate it." With that, she stood and moved to the edge of the porch and slipped her feet into her loud shoes.

"I'm not coming back to work," he told her, intending to send a message through her to his boss. Webber had been relentless about getting Aaron to come in at least one day a week after his leave hit the six-month mark, so he figured he might as well tell him he didn't need to bother this time around. "Not for a while."

Placing her hand on the railing, Mary Beth looked out at the row of sturdy wooden houses that lined the quiet street. "It's a heavy thing to carry around all by yourself," she said, "the responsibility for finding those two girls. Please call me anytime. I just stopped by to let you know I'm here."

Aaron looked down at his mud-encased boots, suddenly feeling the exhaustion from a day of crawling through tangled brush.

"And the chief understands," Mary Beth said. "He wanted me to tell you that your office is waiting for you anytime. You're a good cop—there are a lot of people who can use your help when you're ready to give it."

His head popped back up at her words, all thoughts of exhaustion forgotten as the familiar anger coursed through his body. Damn everyone and their not-so-subtle messages to get over it. As if they knew what it felt like to have your guts torn out, to lose your heart. As if they could just blithely go back to their old lives in the same situation. Sure, they never came out and said it, but they always communicated the same thing: Move on. Get back to work. Be the same reliable working stiff you'd been before... Before.

"Mary Beth, I have a question for you."

She pivoted so she was facing him fully, all ears.

"When do you stop feeling the way I feel? When do you say to yourself, 'Ah, my kid's dead. I think I'll go down to Houlihan's and have myself a beer'?"

Mary Beth blinked, but otherwise, her round face didn't waver from its placid, oh-so-supportive expression.

He opened his mouth, brought his hand up to chest level, splaying his fingers before he let it drop again, uselessly to his side. "You tell Webber," he ground out as he moved away from her, "that I'll come back to work... I'll put my life back together when I find my daughter. And if there's nothing left to put back together when that day comes, then Rosie and I will make a new one. Until then, you should all just consider me dead." He pushed through the door and slammed it shut behind him, before considering how his behavior in the face of Mary

Beth's kindness made him look even more like the sorry son of a bitch he was.

AFTER STARING at his television set for way too long, especially considering that it was off, Aaron pushed himself out of the armchair and slammed out of his too-empty house, grabbing his keys on the way out. Without thinking, he got in his car and drove, barely seeing anything but the stretch of road illuminated by his headlights. He made a few turns by rote, then abruptly pulled over to the curb and shut the car off.

And looked out the window at Sabrina's house.

Don't think, Donovan. Just go.

Before he could talk himself out of it, Aaron got out of the car and headed up the walk to Sabrina's front door. For the second time in twenty-four hours, he rang the bell.

A few seconds later, he heard footsteps, and then the door swung open.

"Aaron!" She blinked in surprise. He'd obviously caught her as she was getting ready for bed—she was dressed in a pair of soft blue drawstring pants and a white fitted T-shirt. Her hair was damp from a recent shower and slicked back, emphasizing the regal, angular structure of her face. She quickly recovered from the shock of seeing him after his colossal display of bad manners this afternoon, and her next words were a lot kinder than he deserved. "Can I help you with something?"

He fiddled with his keys. "I just came…" He paused, feeling like an idiot.

"Look, whatever it is, I'm glad," she said. "I wanted to apolo—"

"I'm sorry," he cut in, wanting to get that out there first. "You were right. I was taking…everything out on you, and that's unfair."

She pulled the door open wider in a tacit invitation to come in. He followed her inside, and they sat in her living room, just as they had this morning. Except instead of anger and tension hanging in the air like thick fog, there was only acceptance and gentleness from her. And he just felt hollow.

The living-room furniture crowded the small room, forcing them to sit close to each other. Instead of being awkward, he found it strangely comforting.

She scooted back in the puffy, oversized chair and tucked her legs under her, picking at the beading on one of her ubiquitous throw pillows. "You don't have to apologize. I mean, with everything you've been through, of course you're not all sweetness and light all the time."

He shook his head, feeling unworthy of her generosity. "It's not your fault. I knew it before you showed me that piece of paper, but—" He threw his hands up in the air and let them fall to his sides once more. "There's no excuse. None."

Tossing her pillow to one side, she leaned forward and grabbed his hands. He jerked back slightly in surprise, but then he stilled, staring at her small brown hands curled around his. It was the first time someone had touched him in ages. At least, the first time they'd tried and he'd let them, and all he knew was that he didn't want her to back away.

"You acted like someone in pain. I knew that." She squeezed his fingers and looked him straight in the eye. "Rosie was the center of your world. You're amazing to keep on breathing, without having to worry about what Miss Manners would say about your behavior." He could only look at her, transfixed, hyper-aware of their hands as the corners of her mouth turned up in a sad smile. "Hey, if it takes a little of that burden away for even a minute, you just come over and yell at me anytime. Consider this a carte blanche invitation."

Out. He had to get out, get away from Sabrina and her golden eyes that could see right through him. Get away from her generous spirit and her fierce friendship. He'd once found her captivating, but now it was all just too much. *Don't think. Don't feel. Get out before everything crashes down around you.* He got up and stumbled toward the door.

"Aaron." She scrambled up and followed him, catching him by the elbow just as he put his hand on the knob. His chest throbbed with the sheer effort it took to breathe, to hold himself together. *Don't think. Don't feel.*

"Aaron, God." Her voice shook, causing him to look up and see the brightness in her eyes. She opened her mouth, closed it again, and then leaned forward and simply wrapped her arms around him.

His breath caught. Her small, solid body

connected with his; he inhaled the clean scent of her hair. And instead of falling apart, he sank into her, letting himself be soothed by her touch, propped up by her strength, just for a minute.

He wanted to tell her everything at that moment—about the first time he'd held his baby daughter in his arms, about how lost he'd felt when Rosie's mother had left them when he was so young and didn't have a clue how to care for a small child, about how trusting his little girl had been, from the first time she squeezed his finger in her chubby, walnut-sized little fist until the day he'd lost her.

"Sometimes," he said hoarsely, "I just wish it would be over, even if I just find her—" He stopped, unable to say the word. "Gone. And then I feel like a selfish, sick bastard who doesn't deserve to get his daughter back."

"It's not selfish," she said, her voice fierce. "You've been through so much. It's not selfish to just want it to stop. You don't deserve this. You don't deserve to feel like this."

She gripped him tighter, holding on as if she needed him as much as he'd let himself need her, just for that moment. He closed his eyes, listened to their breathing, and slowly, gradually, he came back to himself.

"Thank you," he whispered to the top of her head after they'd stood like that for God knows how long. "For everything."

And he pulled out of her arms, as gently as he could. Reaching for her face, he scrubbed away a tear on her cheek with the pad of his thumb.

"Sabrina, I don't feel much anymore," he said softly. "I can't."

She nodded, and he knew she understood. Feel too much, and he'd fall apart—and never be able to put himself back together again. But he did allow himself to lean forward, kissing her forehead with as much reverence and gratitude as he could. She gasped softly.

"Don't think I never wish things could have been different with us." He backed up again, until his hip touched the door, and this time shoved his hands in his pockets, well aware that he was still standing too close to her but unable to move any farther. His hesitation gave her time to reach up and cup his face in her hands, and he wanted to lose himself all over again.

"Anything you need, anytime, come find me," she said. "I'm here. No matter what, I'll always be here."

He covered one of her hands with his own and then took it away from his cheek. He couldn't bring himself to let it go right away, so he just nodded.

"Nothing lasts forever, Aaron. Not even this much grief."

Still holding her hand, he opened the door and took a step outside, then another, until he'd put enough distance between them that her fingers slipped from his own.

Chapter Six

Skylar sent the team to a different location the next morning, giving them less difficult terrain to keep them fresh. Their job was to confine their search for Tara to one of the trails near the place where she'd disappeared—a seventeen-mile loop called, imaginatively, the Kalaloch Falls Trail, just so tourist hikers didn't miss the fact that the smallish but still spectacular Kalaloch Falls sat at the moderate hike's halfway point.

Sabrina felt a pang of regret that they were a few miles out from where Tara's trail had gone cold, but she knew it was the right thing to do—the going would be much easier on a beaten path, ensuring that her team would still have the stamina to continue tomorrow. And the next day. And the day after, if need be.

As she led Alex and Jessie down the path—Aaron hanging back a few feet away from them so they all moved in a diamond pattern—she wondered if they were just postponing the inevitable. She hoped not, but it seemed that unless a miracle happened, it was only a matter of time before Skylar found herself in the same position Sabrina had been in six months earlier, standing in front of the Fishers trying to get up the guts to speak.

The rest of her team may have been thinking along the same lines—what else could explain how uncharacteristically quiet they'd all been, even though the tension between Aaron and herself had all but evaporated after their conversation last night.

Conversation. Yeah, right. Her nerve endings sang every time she thought about holding Aaron close, which so far had been quite a lot, even while each memory from the day before was also accompanied by a flash of white-hot anger over his ever-present loss. It was so unfair, not to know, to doubt that you'd ever know what happened to someone you'd loved.

As for Aaron, the loss of his daughter still

weighed heavily on him, but something small and very subtle had changed, too. She'd seen glimpses of the man she'd known six months ago, opening her car door when she'd pulled up to the parking lot near the trailhead, taking her pack from her and asking how she was, his voice and his eyes gentler than they'd been in a long time.

She wondered what was worse—not knowing, or having the worst kind of closure?

Her eyes growing gummy with fatigue, Sabrina slowed her pace through one of the flat areas that broke up the steep, zig-zagging switchbacks on the trail. When squinching her eyes open and shut a few times didn't clear her vision, she raised her gaze from the ground and stopped altogether.

"Where are you, Rosie?" she murmured under her breath. "You have to be somewhere."

"You say something, boss?" Alex piped up from behind her.

She ignored the question, glancing back at Aaron. "Jess, can you take point for a while?"

"Sure." Taking advantage of the pause,

the blonde moved to the center of the trail and took a swig out of a canteen she carried with her. When Sabrina, weighed down by her thoughts, didn't go to the flank position right away, Jessie handed the canteen to Alex and waited.

Sabrina could feel the weight of Aaron's expectation like a hand between her shoulder blades, and it made her hesitate to give up the lead when he was behind her, watching. There was only one reason he was here—he was hunting down a miracle, one she wasn't sure they could deliver. And she didn't want to put Jessie on point, instead preferring to carry as much of the responsibility for the outcome of the day as she could.

What if Rosie were gone? What if the searchers did eventually find her body, hidden under a pile of leaves or a decaying tarp? What if the four of them found it, here, today, and Aaron had to see his daughter that way?

Please, God, don't let that be how this ends.

"Why don't we rest a minute?" Jessie asked. "You look like you could use it."

Alex rubbed his forehead. "I could use it. I think I'm catching the plague."

Rest. Her neck ached from looking down at the ground, and her eyes were still straining to focus, but she knew she could keep going for at least a little while.

"Actually, I'm okay. I think I can stay here for another hour." She didn't even glance at Jessie's reaction. "Alex, do you need to stop?"

"No, no, I'm good. Stayed out too late last night, probably."

"Okay." She turned around and trudged on, scanning the pine-needle-covered ground and hoping for Aaron's miracle.

"Let me know when you want to switch." Unfazed by Sabrina's abrupt change of plans, Jessie fanned back out behind her. Sabrina nodded in acknowledgement of her offer and kept walking.

The day was uncharacteristically sunny— perfect for kayaking down Hood Canal or heading south to hike up Rainier, the state's tallest peak. A few fat, puffy clouds dotted a clean, bright blue sky that looked as though Maxfield Parrish had painted it his signature blue. A cool breeze rustled through the trees, the sound accompanied only by the team's soft footsteps on the packed-dirt path and the thumps of their walking sticks. Just as she was getting her rhythm back, reaching that place where there was nothing but the trail before them, the cry of a whipporwill shrilled through the air. She barely registered the sound, loud as it was, until the insistent bird called again. And again, sounding almost impatient.

And then she remembered that whippoor-wills didn't live in the Pacific Northwest.

Halting abruptly, she whirled to stare at Aaron.

Behind her, Alex raised his hands and skidded to a stop just before crashing into her. "What the——?"

"Bree?" Jessie turned to see what she was looking at.

Aaron's rifle was off his back and in his hands, his eyes dark and intense even from a distance. He lifted his finger to his lips, signaling to them to be quiet, and then he moved into the trees. Despite the fact that she'd never taken her eyes off his retreating figure, he pretty much vanished in the time it took her to exhale.

"What do we do?" Jessie whispered, her blue eyes open so wide, Sabrina could see a line of white all around the pupils. Clearly, just the thought of Aaron feeling the need to get his gun was enough to spook Jess. And to tell the truth, Sabrina was a little spooked herself. After all, none of them were armed, unless you counted their flimsy aluminum walking sticks, which as weapons were about as effective as a plastic fork in a sword fight.

"Maybe Donovan decided he needed to go hunt wabbits," Alex cracked in a terrible Elmer Fudd impression.

"Shut up, Alex." Jessie poked his leg with the end of her stick. "This is serious."

Sabrina squinted down the trail, scanning the forest behind her once, twice, three times. But even though she was trained to notice small changes in terrain, she couldn't see a thing. Couldn't hear anything other than the normal noises of the forest. No footsteps, no whipporwills, nothing.

He'd told them to be quiet. Did he want them to stay still? Pretend nothing had happened and keep going? Pretend nothing out of the ordinary had happened and take a "break?"

"Just listen," she whispered finally, figuring the best course of action was to wait. She'd never been more grateful that tracking was a team endeavor than at this moment, because standing here alone, waiting for whatever it was that had spooked Aaron to show itself would have terrified her.

She clutched her walking stick tightly with both hands, grinding it into the dirt. Was *he* out there, stalking them, waiting to attack them because they were getting too close to…something?

For so long, the park had been a comfort to her, the mountains a refuge. Now, the rainforest seemed too dark, too dense, the thick canopy choking out too much light. Too many places to hide.

From far off in the distance, she heard Aaron shout.

She took off running toward the sound.

Only to slam into Alex's rock-solid arm when he stuck it in front of her, knocking her walking stick to the ground as he wrapped the other arm around her, catching her in a bear hug. "Let go!" she shouted, but he merely tightened his grip.

He grunted as she struggled to push his arms away. "Bree, you don't know what's out there."

"Aaron—"

"Bree, no." Jessie stepped in front of her and put a calming hand on her shoulder. Sabrina shook it off, glaring at her colleague. Aaron needed their help, and all these two wanted to do was have a committee meeting about how best to proceed.

"Aaron has a big rifle and you—ow!" Alex dropped his arms and rubbed the place where her elbow had connected with his ribs. She grimaced, not having meant to hurt him.

"At least let me go first, would you?" With that, Alex took off running down the path on which Aaron had disappeared, brandishing his flimsy-looking walking stick in front of him.

Freaking men. She could have done that. Sabrina bolted after him, hearing Jessie take off just behind her.

A few yards down, the trail turned sharply to the right, and Alex disappeared from sight once he'd made it around the bend. Not being able to see him made her heart beat that much faster, and she broke out into a full-out sprint, pumping her legs as fast as they could go, batting a few low-hanging pine boughs out of her way. She careened around the curve at full speed, and then skidded to an abrupt halt.

In front of her, Aaron stood over a skinny man in a pair of jeans and a blue flannel shirt, lying on the ground. The stranger was resting on his elbows with his knees bent as if he'd tried to crab-walk away from Aaron—until the detective had planted the muzzle of his rifle directly between the man's eyebrows. Apparently to keep him from shuffling back any farther, Aaron had planted one boot firmly on the man's scrawny chest, which looked like it might cave in from the pressure.

"Whoa, man." Still breathing heavily from the sprint, Alex bent over at the waist and put his hands on his knees, looking a little too tired from his short sprint, given that he did Ironman triathlons on a regular basis. "What's going on?"

Jessie looked at him questioningly. "You okay?" He waved her off, still catching his breath.

Aaron didn't seem to hear Alex's question, his focus zeroed in on the man before him. He was breathing hard—from emotion, not exertion—shoulders rising and falling as he fought for control. Then, suddenly, something in his face shifted— his expression relaxed, grew colder, his deep-set eyes turning into twin chips of ice. He'd wrapped his hands so tightly around the rifle, she could see the tendons in them standing out in sharp relief, but now they, too, relaxed. He looked… Oh, no, he looked like he was about to pull the trigger, and damn the consequences.

"Wait—" She took a step forward.

"Get back, Sabrina." The words were quietly spoken, but the force behind them stopped her like a giant, invisible hand.

The man tried to turn his head out of Aaron's line of fire, but anywhere he moved, Aaron followed with a small, precise movement. "What's your problem, man? I didn't do anything to you!" he squeaked. His eyes nearly crossed as he looked at the rifle muzzle, obviously terrified.

Aaron raised his eyebrows in mock surprise. "Didn't you?"

"Jeez, Donovan, what's going on?" Alex asked, a faint sheen of sweat coating his now-pale face.

"Tell me where she is," Aaron demanded, not taking his eyes off his target.

"Who?" the man shouted back.

"You know who."

The man smacked a palm against the packed dirt of the path, a quick, panicked movement. "No, I don't. Just tell me!"

Aaron moved his boot off the man's chest and onto his throat. When the man started gasping and clawing at the boot, Aaron just pressed down harder.

"You need to tell me where she is now." He kept speaking in the same dreadful, calm voice, even while the man's face turned a deep shade of red. "Or I'll shoot your kneecaps out first, and then I will work my way up until you do."

The man gave a few strangled little grunts, and then Aaron let up slightly on the pressure, enough to allow him to speak. "I've seen you around before. You're a cop," the man rasped, now flat on his back and gripping the sole of Aaron's boot with both hands. "You can't do that. You gonna shoot these people, too?" His eyes darted to Sabrina and her team.

Aaron pressed the muzzle directly against the man's forehead, making a slight indentation in the skin above his brow. "No, but let me tell you something," he hissed, his voice low and dangerous. "I'm a cop with nothing left to lose." He pressed his weight down harder on the man's throat, until his victim could no longer make a sound, his mouth opening and closing like a goldfish that had flipped out of its tank. "Make no mistake—I will shoot you."

"Stop it!" Unable to take the scene in front of her anymore, Sabrina darted forward and crouched down next to the man. She slipped her fingers underneath Aaron's boot, trying to lift it up. It wouldn't budge. "He can't tell you anything if you crush his throat!"

A heartbeat. Another. And then Aaron finally lifted his foot, though the gun stayed in position. The man opened his mouth and gave a loud, shuddering inhale, then flipped onto his stomach, coughing and sputtering into the ground.

Sabrina stood. "Donovan, you tell me what just happened right now, or—"

"There's a jacket," he broke in, still watching the man struggle noisily to regain his breath. "A few feet away from us, by that fallen tree." He jerked his head to the right. Jessie immediately set off in the direction he'd indicated.

A few seconds later, she held up a filthy-looking denim coat, covered with trailing bits of leaves and dried pine needles. Sabrina couldn't tell if it was a child's jacket or one of the cropped adult version that were currently in fashion.

"He dropped it when I was chasing him." And then Aaron's icy facade crumbled suddenly, and the grief was back in full force. "It belongs to my daughter."

SHE HAD NEVER REALIZED what a luxury clocks were until now.

Time. She had no concept of it anymore. It was never daytime in her little room. Just dark, a relentless, maddening dark that pressed against her skin, wrapped around her rib cage and stole her breath. Absorbed her screams.

She fell asleep to it, woke to it, watched

the pictures from her old life against the backdrop it provided. The only break in the dark was when he came in, and she'd take the terrors of her mind any day.

She lay on the lumpy little cot she'd already come to think of as hers, staring into the blackness and wondering if the days had become months yet.

She'd spent the first hours after he'd left her alone feeling her way around the room. That hadn't taken long, considering how small it was. She'd pulled the cot against each of the walls, feeling as high as she could to see if there were any windows, either boarded up or painted over.

There weren't.

The walls felt cool to her touch, as though she was in a basement. The floor was a mercilessly cold concrete, and there was a plastic bucket in the corner for her to use as a toilet. He'd taken her clothes, leaving her a musty-smelling blanket, which she was not allowed to wrap around herself when he came into the room. That she'd learned right away.

There were others. She could hear them sometimes, when he took them all out to listen to his insane ramblings about evolution and overcoming Man, whatever that meant. He'd come for her, putting some kind of bag over her head with zippers over the eyes and mouth, and take her to another room with a row of stalls, like a public shower with no curtains. He'd chain her arms above her head in one of the stalls and unzip the eyeholes, and he'd be standing before her, the others next to her in the other stalls as he marched back and forth in front of the spotlight he'd used on her the first time. It was getting harder and harder to adjust her vision to that brilliance. She worried that when she got out, she'd be half-blind.

The *when* caught in her mind, the word replaying over and over as she trailed the back of her hand back and forth on the cool cinder-block wall. What if it wasn't *when?* What if it was *if?* What if *when* never happened? She giggled suddenly, a panicked, high-pitched sound.

God, she was starting to sound just as crazy as he was.

But on those occasions when he took her out, into the next room, she never saw the others, but she could hear them. They didn't talk, but sometimes they cried. And sometimes, he'd go into a stall with one of them, and they'd make the worst kinds of sounds.

Her breath caught. Don't go there. Don't go there. *Don'tgodon'tgodon'tgo*.

It was so dark. She'd go nuts if she had to stay in this room for another minute. Someone had to hear her. Please someone hear her. Someone walk by. They couldn't still be in the woods, there had to be people nearby.

Panic wrapped around her ribs, tap-tap-tapping on her breastbone. "Help me!" she shouted suddenly, catapulting up from the cot and heading to where she knew the door was. She pounded her fists on it, even though the heavy steel absorbed most of the sound. The dark swallowed the rest.

"Help me! Somebody get us out of here! Somebody hear us!"

One of her fingernails caught in the ridge between the door and the wall. When she jerked her hand up, it ripped off the nail bed, leaving behind a fiery, quick pain.

"Oh, God," she cried, squeezing her finger hard to try to stop the sting. She brought her fingers to her mouth to suck on the damaged one, tasting the sharp tang of blood and raw skin. "Oh, God, get me out. Please get me out. Please, please, please get me out." Leaning her forehead against the door, she sank to the floor, the sudden burst of frantic energy draining away with the pain. How many times would she do this? How many times would she bang her body against the walls of this room before it stopped mattering to her anymore?

Sometimes, she wished he'd just kill her. Okay, maybe most of the time she wished that. This was so much worse than dying.

She didn't know how long she sat there, quietly crying, but all of a sudden she heard something unfamiliar, a skittering of stones behind her that had her struggling to get herself back under control. He always came through the door, so what the heck was that?

Her first thought was that it was a mouse that had somehow made its way into her room, maybe through the drain in the floor. Maybe she could catch it and make it her pet. She'd have someone to talk to, like that dude had had his volleyball in that movie where his plane had crashed on a deserted island.

Taking a deep, shuddering breath, she

swiped at her damp face with the back of one hand and moved toward the sound.

"Hello?" someone whispered.

Oh my God. Was someone here? Were they rescuing her? She moved to the other side of the room and fell to her knees, feeling frantically along the wall for the opening through which she'd heard the voice. "In here! I'm in here!"

"Shh!" the voice admonished in a harsh whisper. "So am I. You have to be quiet."

Not a rescuer. Just one of them. The others.

Fat lot of good that did her. She felt herself getting irrationally angry with the voice, as if she were standing somewhere outside herself watching herself act irrationally. But the voice was just as stuck as she was, and she had to be angry at someone.

"What's your name?" the voice demanded.

She didn't say anything.

"Come on, what's your name? It's okay."

"Tara," she said begrudgingly.

"You're the new one, right? The one he just brought in?"

Just. It seemed like a whole lifetime ago.

"I guess. Who are you?" she whispered. Her fingers found the opening in the wall, a jagged hole a few inches from the floor. The edges crumbled slightly when she touched them.

"I'm Rosie."

Tara sat up. "Rosie Donovan?" Rosie was a couple of years behind her in school, so she hadn't known her well, but the whole school knew when she'd gone missing.

But that had been months ago.

Her chest heaved, and she could hear her own breathing in her ears, drowning out whatever else Rosie was saying. Months ago. Months in this place. Months with him.

"Tara? Tara, calm down. You've gotta pull it together. Tara?"

Okay. Okay, she could do this. She could stop freaking out, because what if Rosie left her and she was all alone again? She sniffled, grabbing the blanket off her nearby bed and wrapping it around herself. Which was ridiculous, given that Rosie couldn't see her, but it made her feel a little better. "I'm here. How did you make this hole?"

"My bed has springs. I pried one of them

loose and started chipping at the wall," she whispered.

Somewhere in the back of her brain, the spark of an idea ignited. "Can I see it?" Tara's own cot had strips of tightly woven canvas holding up the smelly mattress, not springs. "I want to make the hole on my side bigger."

"Here." A few seconds later, the end of a rusty bedspring poked through the hole. Tara could feel the jagged metal tip where Rosie had pulled the spring free from the rest of her bed's foundation. "Maybe you can start one on the other side and see if there's someone there."

Yeah, maybe. But she wasn't planning to be here for that long.

From the other side of the wall, she heard Rosie gasp. "He's at my door!" she hissed. "Use your blanket to cover the hole. And whatever you do, don't—"

But the rest of her words were muffled, as she heard Rosie shuffle away. She dropped her blanket in a pile near the hole, making sure that it was concealed, but she kept the spring in her hand, curling her fingers tightly around it.

A few minutes later, the door opened. She flinched and turned her head, shutting her eyes tightly at the brightness from his lantern.

"Hello, little bird."

She pressed her lips together tightly to keep herself from sobbing out loud. Her dad always called her "little bird." She didn't know how this creep knew that, or how long he'd watched her to find out.

She felt him fitting the hood over her head. Almost immediately, her face flushed from the heat, sweat causing her skin to stick to the thick, vinyl-like material. Pretty soon, the air inside wouldn't be quite enough, and she'd be sucking on the zipper over her mouth, trying to draw in enough oxygen through it.

"Kneel."

Oh, no. She started to but then shook her head, curling her arms across her chest and then bowing over her folded legs. No, no, no, no.

She felt him move closer to her. "Kneel."

No, no, no, no.

Gripping her chin tightly with one hand, he raised her face up at a painful angle and unzipped the opening over her mouth. She inhaled deeply through it.

"Kneel."

She heard a deep, keening sound and wondered if it was coming from her.

He wrapped something around her neck, pulled tightly so she had no air, until the pressure was so intense, brightly colored lights danced in front of her eyes. She clawed at her neck, feeling the leather cords cutting off her air but unable to loosen them.

Then the pressure eased, and she inhaled noisily, greedily, collapsing on the ground and coughing into the cold, hard floor.

He laughed softly. The whip he'd wrapped around her neck was still there— she could smell the leather, knew the creaking sound it made when he squeezed it. She felt its insistent tug once more.

"Kneel."

She stilled her breathing, willed herself to calm down, do what she needed to do to survive. Bracing herself with one hand, she knelt.

The whip slackened, and she felt it uncoil and slither off her skin. He moved closer, until she could feel the hairs of his legs on her bare arm.

She brought her hand up, the hand that

still held the bedspring, and plunged the jagged metal end into his thigh.

"I hope you die of tetanus, you perv."

Tara pulled the hood off her head and took off running.

Chapter Seven

"He looks so normal." Jessie worried her lower lip with her teeth as she peered through the window in Skylar's office at the ranger station. Outside, Aaron and his partner, Detective Eddie Ventaglia, were walking the man they'd brought off the ridge into Ventaglia's tan Crown Victoria.

Sabrina folded her arms and considered Jessie's statement. Now that the guy—Dean Witkowski, according to Ventaglia—was walking rather than lying on his back pleading for his life, he did look normal—disturbingly so. A little too thin, but he had a completely unremarkable face, average blue eyes, average nose, and a not-too-prominent, not-too-sunken chin framed in a dark, neatly trimmed goatee. His medium-brown hair was seriously thinning on top, a fact that he'd unsuccessfully tried to remedy with a spiky haircut and a little too much hair gel. Honestly, she not only wouldn't have looked twice at the guy, she doubted she'd remember much about him once she looked away. He'd had no prior run-ins with the law—just an average, unremarkable citizen who might or might not be disguising something rotten in his core. They watched as Ventaglia pushed down on the guy's head, forcing him to crouch and fold himself into the back seat of the car.

"Oooh." Jessie flinched as Aaron pounded his fist on the vehicle's roof in obvious frustration once he'd closed the door behind Witkowski. Ventaglia started to say something, presumably about the possible damage Aaron had just inflicted on his car, and then stopped himself when he saw Aaron's face.

"Guess Donovan's going to be playing bad cop when they question him at the station, hmmm?" Sidling closer to Sabrina's left side to get a better look, Skylar scrubbed both hands through her trendy razored haircut, causing the short red strands to stick up where her fingers had been.

"He's been doing that since he saw this guy." Jessie brought her hand to her mouth and started gnawing absently on one of her fingernails.

"Can you blame him?" Skylar asked.

Sabrina couldn't. Not after seeing that sleazy little man holding Rosie's jacket. Six months after the girl had disappeared wearing it.

Too bad Witkowski wasn't the kidnapper.

"So, you're sure this isn't the guy who took Tara?" Skylar turned away from the window and leaned against the back of her desk.

"I'm sure," Sabrina replied. "Mr. Witkowski's foot is a good three sizes larger than the man who took Tara off the ridge." Anyone could wear shoes that were too big for his feet, but it would be really difficult to go three sizes smaller. "He also showed considerable wear patterns on the outside edges of his soles."

"Ah, yes, I noticed the lovely gentleman seemed a little bowlegged," Skylar noted.

"Right. And the prints we found next to Tara's didn't have that kind of wear."

"He could still know something." Jessie

started to bite her thumbnail, then looked down and glared at it, dropping her hand abruptly. "Stupid, nasty habit."

"I hope he does." Skylar looked back outside again, to where Aaron and Eddie were in deep discussion. "Maybe those two can squeeze something out of him."

They could only hope.

Just then, a tan-and-green mini-SUV pulled into the lot, completely obscuring the two detectives from sight. The driver's-side door opened, and a woman with shoulder-length black hair streaked with silver got out.

"Janie Fisher," Jessie muttered. "Oh, no."

"It's okay. I got it." The last thing she needed right now was to deal with a frantic, desperate parent, but Sabrina knew that what she needed paled in comparison with what Janie Fisher needed. She turned and headed out of Skylar's office and toward the ranger-station doors.

Janie met her just as she pushed her way outside. She probably didn't even realize just how hard she'd gripped Sabrina's elbow to get her attention. "Sabrina, please, do you have a moment?"

Sabrina put her hand over Janie's. "Of course, Janie." She didn't know the woman well, but Janie and her husband owned the small grocery store that she often shopped at, and they were friendly enough to be on a first-name basis. "Would you like to come inside?"

Janie shook her head. "No. No, this won't take long. I just wanted to know, is it true, what they're saying? That the person responsible for Rosie Donovan's disappearance might have taken my Tara?"

Sabrina hesitated. Port Renegade was a small town disguised as a city in so many ways. Tell Janie the truth, and it would spread like a cloud of noxious gas. And she wasn't sure that's what Aaron and the police department wanted at this point.

"No one's sure about that, Janie. We're just looking at all of the possibilities." Not for the first time, she wished so much that she could find Tara and bring her home. No mother should have to go through this.

"But it's possible?" Janie pushed her long hair away from her face, the faintest glimmer of suppressed hysteria in her red-rimmed eyes.

"I don't know," Sabrina said truthfully. "We're looking into that."

"Sabrina, I thought I could count on you

to level with me," Janie snapped, planting her hands on her hips. "This is a small city. Everyone's talking about why Aaron Donovan went on leave less than a week after he came back on duty."

When Sabrina didn't say anything, she continued, her voice pleading, "I just want to know what's going on. She's my daughter. Why can't you find her?"

Sabrina closed her eyes. *Oh, please, not again. Not again. I can't do this again.* "Janie," she said, looking at the woman once more, "I'm doing my best. We all are. I promise you that."

Steepling her hands in front of her trembling mouth, Janie obviously struggled to keep herself under control. "I know. I know. I just…I feel so helpless, you know?"

Sabrina did know. And really, she would have rather run away screaming than deal with Janie's grief, because it just reminded her of her own failures. Girl gets lost in the woods, she finds girl. Why couldn't it just be that simple?

"When will you stop looking?"

Pulling herself out of her thoughts, Sabrina started in surprise. "I'm sorry, what?"

"I don't want to be confrontational. I just want to know. I remember when you called the search for that Donovan girl." And then the tears that Janie had been keeping back started to flow down her cheeks unchecked. "I just wanted to know at what point you would stop looking."

"Janie, I—" She stopped, unable to utter the promise she wanted to give the woman. What happened if another week went by? Two weeks? She couldn't promise to keep SAR tied up when other people needed their help. Just like last time, it was impractical to keep on going when you'd reached a dead end.

Janie looked at her expectantly. The whole outburst had probably been to exact a promise out of her that she'd never be able to keep.

Sabrina took a deep breath. "Whatever happens, in the worst-case scenario, if we don't find Tara, we'll never stop looking. Janie, even if you hear that officially we have, I promise, every single one of our searchers will be keeping an eye out for her every time we're on that trail."

Janie reached out and gripped Sabrina's hand. "Really?"

"You have my word."

She nodded, several times, obviously unable to speak. And then, "I'll hold you to that."

"You can."

With that, Janie got into her SUV and drove off. Eddie's car was no longer behind it.

Feeling drained, Sabrina sank down on the front step to the ranger station once Janie's vehicle was out of sight. A few minutes later, someone sat down beside her. Figuring it was Skylar or Jessie, she turned...and came face-to-face with Aaron.

She blinked in surprise. "What are you doing here?"

Resting his forearms on his knees, he gave her a little half smile, then looked away. "Saw Janie. Figured I'd see if you're all right."

"But—" she began, confused. "Don't you want to be downtown with Witkowski?" She knew he must be dying to question the man about that jacket.

Aaron's face darkened at the man's name, and he stared off into the distance. "Eddie wanted to let him sit for a while in the interrogation room. Sometimes, it wears them down enough that they'll get to the truth a little faster than if you go at them right away."

"Ah."

"Did anything ever come of the tire tread we found?" It was sort of a random question, but she figured she could use a little good news right now, if the track had proven to be a useful clue.

He shook his head, quickly dashing her hopes. "It's a standard-size Goodyear tire that fits on hundreds of sedan-style vehicles. If we find his vehicle, we can compare it to the track to put him at the scene, but that's about it."

She sighed, and then the two of them sat in companionable silence for a moment.

"I know where she is right now. It's the worst feeling in the world." Aaron picked up a pebble off the ground, then stood and threw it. A few seconds later, Sabrina heard it crash into the thick greenery on the far side of the lot. She knew he was talking about Janie. "Don't let her get to you."

Sabrina remained seated, hugging her knees. "But I understand what she's saying. It seems like it should be simple. Someone gets lost, we should find them." And then, suddenly, all of her pent-up emotions came perilously close to the surface, and she had to struggle to hold them back, to swallow her frustration so she could speak again. "Why can't we find them?"

He spun around, and before she knew it, she was in his arms. He stroked her hair while she clung to him, and dammit if she didn't start to cry.

"Aaron, I never cry." She buried her face in the warmth between his neck and shoulder, tears flowing down her face and dampening his shirt.

"I know."

They remained like that for a while, him sitting there, rock-solid, and her crying all over the place, trying to muffle the sounds by pressing her face against him, breathing in the scent of the soap he used and the laundry detergent in his clothes mingled with the scent of a good, healthy sweat from hiking. She wondered vaguely whether Skylar or Jessie had seen her clinging to the man, and then she realized she didn't care. Everyone was entitled to cave under pressure for a little bit, and today was her day.

She took a deep breath, swiped at her

eyes, and straightened, her arms still on Aaron's shoulders, her body still all too aware of how close he was, how his arms were still around her waist, his fingers in her hair. She didn't realize that he'd taken the rubber band out of it until she felt a release of tension at the back of her head, and then her hair falling around her shoulders.

"Your hair is beautiful when it's down," he murmured.

She couldn't help it. She put her palms on his shoulders, then leaned forward, craning her neck and pressing her lips gently to his.

His mouth was warm, and soft, and just as sweet as she remembered. She also remembered just how much passion he could put into his kiss, and how, even though they hadn't slept together, he'd still set her on fire.

Wow, how disrespectful. The man had lost his daughter, for heaven's sake, and all she could think of was… She pulled back, unable to look at him. "Aaron, I'm sorry. That was—"

"Just what I needed." He put his hand under her chin and tipped her face upward. "It's okay to wish things were the way they were before." She didn't have to ask before what. "I wish it all the time, every damn day." He leaned forward once more, brushing her cheek with his lips. "Every time I see you." His breath was warm on her skin, and she closed her eyes, savoring the moment she knew would be gone too quickly.

"I was going to say 'incredibly selfish,'" she murmured. And speaking of selfish, despite her good intentions, she couldn't seem to let him go, her arms still around his neck, fingers tangling in the soft hair at his collar.

He laughed softly, intimately. It was the closest she'd seen him to being normal, being almost happy since Rosie had disappeared. His lips brushed hers once more, and then it was he who pulled back. The spark that had been in his eyes dimmed, quickly replaced by the sadness that overshadowed him like dense fog. "I have to go, Sabrina."

She nodded, swallowed. "I know."

She dropped her hands. He turned away.

"Aaron?" she called, after he'd only gotten a few feet from her. "Thanks." Whether Eddie wanted to wait or not, she knew it had cost him to stay behind, rather than going to the police station immediately for the interrogation.

He nodded. "You bet."

"SO, TELL ME how you got that jacket." Detective Eddie Ventaglia leaned back in his metal-and- fabric chair, folding his hands across the slight paunch under his pale blue dress shirt. Eddie was tall—well over six feet—and broad, so he always looked slightly off-balance on normal-sized furniture.

Dean Witkowski leaned forward in his own chair, his cuffed hands resting on his spread knees. "I found it. I was hiking the trails shortly after Rosie Donovan disappeared, and it was just sitting there, stuck on a rock near the edge of this stream. I could sense that it was hers."

From his position behind the one-way glass, observing Ventaglia in action, Aaron snorted. Right.

"Dean." Eddie shook his head, frowning in exaggerated disappointment. "Dean, Dean, Dean. The photo of Rosie we released to the media showed her wearing that jacket. You expect me to buy this? I'm trying to help you."

"Shh—" Witkowski let the curse taper off, unfinished. "Look, Detective, I'm dying for a cigarette. Couldn't I have just one?"

"You tell me what I need to know, and I'll let you smoke yourself into an iron lung, right now," Eddie replied genially.

Witkowski bowed his head, shaking it back and forth, as if to music only he could hear. "Man, I really need a cigarette," he said.

"Tell you what, Dean." Eddie shuffled around in his seat, reaching into the inner breast pocket of his jacket to produce the crumpled pack of Marlboros he kept there for just such occasions. "I'll give you one, but if my supervisors see me doing this, I'm toast." He leaned forward, holding his hand up to his mouth as if he was about to impart a secret. "Boss is one of those health-nut types." He held the pack out, and Dean grabbed it with greedy hands, shaking a cigarette out and putting it between his lips.

"So, how did you get it? Did you meet her on the trails?" Eddie produced a lighter and started flicking the hinged cap open and shut, keeping it tantalizingly out of Witkowski's reach. Dean eyed it expectantly.

"No, man," he said, the cigarette bouncing with each word. "I told you, I just found the jacket."

"Why didn't you turn it in?"

Placing his hands on the table, Witkowski started rapping on the tabletop with his knuckles, obviously growing a little agitated. "Look, are you going to light this thing, or not?"

Ed, don't lose him. Not now, when he was starting to trust you. Just from observing, Aaron had already read Witkowski's baseline—his range of normal behaviors and mannerisms. Deviations from that baseline could mean that the subject was lying. The knuckle-rapping wasn't a deviation, but it was a clear indicator that Witkowski was getting upset and starting to shut down.

As if on cue, Eddie reached over and lit the man's cigarette. "Sure, Dean." He snapped the lighter shut and regarded the other man with his trademark hangdog expression, his brow furrowed and his thick lower lip jutting out slightly. "But I want you to know you're looking at some serious charges of withholding evidence, obstructing a crime scene. You already admitted you know the jacket was Rosie's. And if we find out you had something to do with Rosie's disappearance…" He trailed off, clicking his tongue. "You know, I can get you a good deal but you gotta give me something to work with."

Witkowski exhaled a cloud of smoke, looking a little worried.

"We know someone else was involved, Dean. The trackers found another set of footprints. Did he talk you into coming with him the day she disappeared? Was it all his idea?" When Witkowski didn't answer, Eddie continued spinning his theory. "Did he do something to Rosie? Maybe something you didn't approve of? Maybe you were just having a little fun, and things got out of hand? I know how that can happen."

Aaron clenched his right hand into a tight fist, the stark, brutal images behind Eddie's implications playing mercilessly in his mind. *It's someone else they're talking about. Not my daughter. It's not my daughter*.

"Did you hurt her, Dean? Even if you didn't mean to?"

Witkowski shook his head emphatically, leaning forward to stub out the cigarette in the ashtray Eddie had pushed toward him. "Stop, okay? Just stop. I'll tell you the truth, but you won't believe me."

Aaron held his breath, waiting.

Eddie put his hands on the table, mirroring Witkowski's own movement. "Try me."

"I'm psychic."

Hell. Refraining at the last minute from slamming his palm against the one-way glass, Aaron pushed off it silently and spun around, pacing to the other side of the room. Psychic. Bloody, freaking hell, the guy had to be playing them. He knew several cops who swore by a trusted psychic in their city who assisted with missing persons cases, but if Witkowski was psychic, then he was Harry Freaking Potter.

"That's not going to help me help you, Dean," Eddie replied with what was some seriously impressive patience. If Aaron had been in there, he'd have been tempted to illegally smack the man's head into the table until he made sense. Which was pretty much why Eddie had insisted that Aaron stay outside the interrogation room.

Dead end. Another dead end.

"No, really." Witkowski cupped his hands in front of him, as if holding the sides of a small bowl. "I mean, I'm not that great at it, but—"

"A not-so-great psychic. Just what the world needs," Aaron snarled at the glass, sinking into his anger because there just wasn't any other option, other than losing it completely.

"—I'm right more often than I'm wrong. Especially if I have an object, like the jacket." He sat back in the chair and shrugged. "I just thought if I took the jacket around the trails, I'd eventually get a hit. And when I saw the searchers going up after this Tara Fisher thing, I figured I'd follow them and see if anything…" He trailed off.

"Rang any of your psychic bells." Eddie sighed.

Witkowski's shoulders drooped a little at the doubt in Eddie's voice. "Pretty much," he said to the floor.

A knock on the door interrupted the proceedings. Not that there was much to interrupt—Witkowski's baseline was still solid as a rock. He obviously believed he was psychic, and whether he knew anything else about the girls who had disappeared was something that could take days to pry out of him.

"Come in!" Eddie snapped, apparently feeling the same frustration that was gnawing at Aaron's gut.

At the same time, the door to the observation room opened, and Brenda Kessler, another detective in the homicide division, stepped inside. "Aaron, another girl just went missing inside the park," she said without preamble. He felt the chill of her words down to his bones.

"Who?"

"I'll fill you in on the way to the chopper pad. Sabrina Adelante and her team are already in the area, and they're sending a chopper to come and take you to them." Kessler was already halfway out the door when she turned. "They said to bring your rifle."

Chapter Eight

Tara bolted through the door, the man's angry howl ringing in her ears. She knew that taking a bedspring in his leg wasn't going to slow him down much, so she had to make every second of her advantage count.

The spotlight he'd shone in her room was still on, illuminating her way. She'd seen the door before, the one he used to come in and out while they were chained up in their stalls, and she headed for it.

Her hands smacked against the cool metal, and she fumbled for the knob, turning it, and then she was through.

Not three feet from the first door, another one stood, also steel, with a small, dirty glass-and-chicken-wire window through which she could only see darkness. Tara launched herself at the door, grabbing the handle and twisting it. When it refused to give more than a few millimeters, she rattled the knob in her hand, already knowing that it was locked.

"Oh, God, open, please open, please, please, open," she sobbed. She could hear him walking across the large room. His steps were slow, measured, as if he were taking his time, completely unworried that she'd escape. Fumbling with her other hand along the door frame, she tried to figure out what was holding the door shut and keeping her from getting out.

Her fingers closed around a thick padlock, with a series of six tumblers that needed to be turned in the correct combination for the lock to open.

She was trapped.

She dropped the lock and cried out as the inner door opened. He grabbed her from behind, pressing his mouth against her ear and making her want to crawl out of her skin. She struggled against him, but he held her fast.

"Where are you going, little bird?" he murmured, his hands moving up the sides of her waist, across her stomach. He laughed softly at her obvious distress as she squirmed in a futile attempt to get away from him. "You don't belong to yourself anymore."

Gasping in revulsion each time he touched her, she tried to push his hands away, to get him off her, but he was relentless, and she knew she was only making him angry.

"I'm the only person in the world who knows that combination. If something happened to me, all three of you would die in here." He reached back and cracked her across the face with the back of his hand. She fell to the ground, pain blooming all along her right jaw and cheekbone, and she curled up into a ball, whimpering in fear and pain and hating herself for it. Hating him even more.

"Think about that next time you try to run."

"THIS IS like a nightmare." Jessie looked up through the towering pines at the sky, which was starting to take on the golden cast of late afternoon. Too much longer, and they'd be in the dark.

Not that it was impossible to search at night, but it sure made life more difficult.

Especially since they were down by one—
the uncomfortable symptoms Alex had dis-
played earlier that morning had quickly
morphed into a nasty case of the flu.
Although he'd tried to stay on his feet,
Skylar had taken one look at his clammy
face and had sent him home.

"Maybe she's just an ordinary lost
hiker," Sabrina replied, doubting her own
words even as she uttered them. Jessie's
sigh told her she didn't believe them either.

The "she" in question was Jennifer
Jenkins, a University of Seattle sophomore
who'd been spending her weeklong fall
break on a remote camping trip in the
Olympics with her boyfriend. The two had
hiked for a couple of days on Mosley Gap
Trail, a faint path heading northwest that
ended 2,200 feet up Samson Ridge on the
banks of a clear mountain stream that would
eventually empty into the Dungeness River.
Setting up their tent in the lush, near-pristine
location where few hikers had recently
been, the two had been roughing it together
in the great outdoors for the past week.

Because the campsite was so far out,
Jessie and Sabrina had been ferried to it via
SAR helicopter, which Port Renegade

shared with a couple of nearby state parks. The pilot would be working overtime for the rest of the day and possibly into the night, dropping search teams at various points around Mosley Gap to assist. Skylar had called in favors from SAR units as far off as Snoqualmie to get more helicopters to join the search. In such a remote location, they'd need them just to relay radio transmissions so they could communicate with Skylar at the base.

Sabrina crouched down near the small river's bank, the water gurgling softly as it rolled past at a leisurely pace. She took in the flurry of sign that Jennifer and her boyfriend had left in the sand and rocks during their three days at the site, able to assess the routine they'd fallen into of fishing, cooking, washing up and lounging around without too much effort. But it was going to take a while to separate old tracks from new and figure out which way Jennifer had gone last night.

Several feet away, Jessie checked out the tracks near the pair's bright blue tent, which was still set up near a patch of black-eyed Susans, their sunny orange and yellow petals tilted toward the sky. The tent's pointed roof had started to sag a little from the nightly rainfall, water pooling in the droopiest portions. A circle of heavy gray rocks surrounded the cold pile of ashes that had been the couple's campfire.

Apparently, Jennifer had left the tent the night before to wash up in the river and hadn't returned. After a sleepless night of stumbling around in the dark with only his lantern for company, her boyfriend had spent the entire day hauling himself back to civilization as quickly as he could to get help. He'd made it to the ranger station, filthy, scratched up and nearly falling down from exhaustion, just a few minutes after Jessie and Sabrina came back from their lunch break. Skylar hadn't exactly been excited about sending the two of them back out, especially with Alex down, but since the rest of the search teams were either on Renegade Ridge looking for Tara or on their day off, she'd agreed to do so until more could be called in.

"Bree, over here!"

Pushing herself off the rocky riverbank with her fingertips, Sabrina stood and headed for Jessie, scanning the ground as she went, just in case something out of place caught her eye.

"Check that out." Jessie pointed to a thick patch of stinging nettle tangled together with some brushy-looking pigweed. "See how that nettle over there is broken, like someone plowed through it?"

As they moved closer to the poisonous plants, Sabrina took in the one bristly stalk bent at a severe angle, her skin itching at the mere idea of touching the hair-thin stinging barbs. "Who would walk into a patch of nettle, unless they had no other choice?"

"Exactly."

Fortunately, the nettle appeared to be contained to this one bunch, so they wouldn't have to wade through it themselves to follow the trail. "Maybe the boyfriend got into it when he was looking for her in the dark, but it's worth checking out."

Sabrina and Jessie navigated around the plants, giving them a wide, respectful berth. Sabrina had accidentally grabbed on to nettle once, as a kid, and the feeling that someone had burned her hand while simultaneously using it as a pincushion wasn't one she'd ever forget. Once they were safely away from the stinging plants, Jessie quickly picked up the trail of who or whatever had pushed through them. Even though the undergrowth thinned out here, the sign was easy to follow—mashed leaves, bent grasses, freshly turned earth, a heel curve or toe impression here and there. Every once in a while, they'd even spot a partial print.

"Same story—she was being chased by someone, and it wasn't her boyfriend," Sabrina murmured. Jessie, meanwhile, used her walking stick to take a rough measurement of Jennifer's stride interval.

"She's definitely running. These prints are much farther apart than the ones at the campsite." Jessie pitched the end of her stick into the ground and used it as leverage to help her stand. "You don't know how much I was hoping she was just plain lost."

"No, I think I do." Sabrina felt sick at the thought of what they'd find once the trail ended. She scanned the tracks until she found a complete footprint in a patch of dirt surrounding the rough trunk of a western hemlock. Setting her backpack on the ground, she crouched down on the needle-strewn ground, batting a couple of the hemlock's nickel-sized pine cones out of the way with the back of her hand.

"His?" Jessie asked.

"I think so. Look at the zigzag pattern." Sure enough, the marks made by the boot matched the partial prints they had of the person who'd been with Rosie when she'd disappeared, and who'd carried Tara down Renegade Ridge. Just to be sure, Sabrina got a measuring tape out of her pack to confirm an exact match.

"What the hell was he doing over here?" she muttered. The other girls had been taken on the trails close to the park entrance. Mosley Gap Trail was as remote as you could go on this side of the rainforest without getting off the trails and illegally mashing through protected areas. She stretched the tape across the length of the print, and then the width.

It was a match, all right.

Behind her, she heard Jessie murmur something, but the words didn't register. Holy mother of God, how long had this guy followed Jennifer and her boyfriend? How long had he been watching them, before he got the perfect opportunity to attack?

Sitting back on her heels, she pushed the small button that retracted the measuring tape into its metal case with a zip.

"You know, if there was ever a day that I missed Alex…" Letting the sentence trail off, she recorded the measurements in the small notebook she also carried in her pack, then swapped both it and her measuring tape for the digital camera. "We should head back. Even women as intimidating as we are shouldn't be out here—" Bracing herself with one hand on the tree, the scaly red bark digging into her skin, she stood and turned to Jessie.

Who wasn't there.

"—alone." She turned in a slow circle, scanning the silent forest. "Jess?"

No answer.

Okay, don't panic. Jessie had been right behind her just a few seconds ago—she couldn't have gone far. Sabrina snapped a couple of quick photos of the footprint, then picked up her pack again and walked around the large tree. Pushing a strand of low-hanging moss out of her way, she ducked under a branch, mentally kicking herself for not listening to the last thing Jessie had said.

And then she wanted to kick Jessie for leaving her anyway. She didn't even care if the woman had had to pee—it was becoming all too clear that hiking in the woods without Aaron's giant assault rifle to keep them company was dangerous.

"Jess?"

She usually found hiking alone in the park peaceful, soothing. Some people found the ocean rejuvenating, but she'd always found her bliss in the mountains. But this time, the silence that followed her shout felt oppressive instead.

"Jessie, for heaven's sake, will you get back here?"

A twig snapped behind her, and Sabrina whirled to face the sound.

"Jess?" she whispered to the swirl of dry leaves and pine needles blowing through the trees.

Don't freak out. Don't freak out. Don't freak out.

Go or stay? Her decision right now could haunt her for the rest of her life, if she made the wrong one. Did she keep following the trail in the hopes that Jessie would do the same and they'd meet each other at some point? Or did she get back to the ranger station to get assistance—or, at least, get to an area where she could use their radio?

But if Jessie needed help, Sabrina was pretty much the only one in a position to provide it at the moment. Knowing Skylar as she did, the nearest team was probably three or four miles out and heading away from her.

Her hand went to her radio, even as she told herself it wouldn't work. She was tempted to try anyway, but then again, she didn't want to attract any more attention to herself with a blare of radio static…if there was someone else out here with them.

Then again, if this all wasn't Jessie's idea of a joke—and she well knew that Jess didn't have that kind of cruel sense of humor—it didn't matter. Anyone intending to do her harm would probably know where she was already.

She held her body completely still, breathing as slowly and quietly as possible, taking in her surroundings just by moving her eyes, like a cornered rabbit hoping the fox wouldn't see it if it just didn't move.

Stop acting like a victim. You're not one yet.

To her right, a stand of paper-barked birch trees mixed in with the thick trunks of old-growth Sitka spruce trees. Nothing looked out of the ordinary.

A tracker's trained to notice anomalies in her surroundings. If he's here, you should see him.

To her left lay the crumbling trunk of a Douglas fir that had toppled long ago. The tree had lived for so many centuries, the trunk's width was greater than her height.

Since she didn't know what the fallen tree was blocking, she shifted gears and listened for anything outside the ordinary sounds of the rainforest. Nothing stood out, beyond the soothing hiss of the wind blowing through the pine boughs, the songs of a hundred different birds, the crackle of dry deciduous leaves as they swirled around the ground.

So far, so good.

Straight ahead, more evergreens, thick and wild and draped with moss, with brushy ferns and tangling vines curling around the base of them.

Still nothing. Other than that one twig snapping, she couldn't sense another person or even an animal in the vicinity.

Which way?

And then she heard it—the faintest rustling behind the fallen tree. It could have been a snake, a fox. But somehow, she knew, she just knew it wasn't.

Sabrina's heart hammered into triple time. Slowly backing up, she trailed her fingers along the trunk of the Sitka spruce just for the comfort of touching something. She didn't want to turn her back on whoever that was, didn't want him to catch her by surprise. Dammit, she didn't want to be a victim.

Behind the fallen trunk, something started to rise.

Move.

She dropped her walking stick and bolted in the opposite direction, not caring that she didn't know who or what had been behind the tree. If Jessie was getting all Washington Chainsaw Massacre on her, she deserved to be left alone. And if it wasn't Jessie…

Sabrina crashed through the woods, operating on pure instinct as she headed back toward the campsite. But as she passed the first of the crepe-paper flags she and Jessie had laid to mark their trail, she knew getting out into the open would put her at a distinct disadvantage if what followed her wasn't benign.

Keep to the trees. You know these parklands better than anyone.

She caught a movement out of the corner of her eye, and turned her head as something wove through the trees on a parallel course, easily keeping up with her stride for stride. He was all in black, making him look like a giant spider as he swooped around and under the trees, grabbing branches and using them to propel himself forward even faster. But instead of heading toward her, he stayed a few yards away, content to stalk her for now.

Her legs felt heavy with the fatigue of hiking all day, and she gave a frustrated yell at the effort it took to keep going. She hooked left, pushing herself to go faster as she glanced toward her pursuer once more.

Her inattention cost her. Her foot hooked under a tree root, and she stumbled. The panic in her chest bloomed into something huge, suffocating. Frantically windmilling her arms, she tried desperately to regain her balance, to keep going. Fall now, and it was all over.

Catching a low-hanging branch with her hand, she steadied herself. She yanked her foot free and took off again.

Eyes on the ground, Adelante.

"Jessie!" she shouted. Of course there was no response.

When the ground grew more level, she looked left again. The man was still on his parallel track, although he'd moved a little closer. Close enough for her to see that he wore a ski mask over his face.

Why was it that ski masks never meant some-thing good?

He smiled at her when he noticed her look, and she turned away, kept pushing on. A game. This was all a goddamned game for him. He was toying with her. *Well, you don't know who you're messing with, bucko. I can run for days if I have to.*

She batted a branch out of her way just before it hit her in the face. Oh, God, he was tall. She might have the endurance of a marathon runner, but there was no way she had the speed to elude someone with that long stride.

Not that she wasn't going to try.

She changed course again, using her un-failing sense of direction to adjust her path to the southwest, toward Mosley Gap. If she could get there, where a bunch of trails intersected...

She could lose him. Her radio might work.

"Sssabrina!"

It was a loud whisper. And the fact that he knew her name terrified her.

The terrain shifted suddenly beneath her feet, turning into a gradual downward slope. Looking ahead, she could see exactly where the slope ended in an abrupt edge. Cliff or navigable incline? She had no idea.

On a gamble, she headed for it. The man who'd called her name turned as well, still staying parallel. When she reached the drop-off, she grabbed a small sapling and used it for leverage while she made a split-second assessment—and then hurled herself over the edge.

Her boots slipped and slid down the steep mountainside, raining small showers of loose dirt with her every step. The incline was so sharply angled, all she had to do was reach out, and she'd touch the ground behind her even from a standing position.

Behind her, she could hear him crashing

down the mountainside after her. Grabbing on to a thick weed for balance, she jumped down a near-vertical stretch. Her ankle turned at the impact when she hit the ground, but she ignored the pain and kept going.

As soon as she got to the bottom, she tore into the trees, operating on instinct. She couldn't hear anything other than her jagged gasps for air and the blood pounding in her ears. Once she'd been running for a while, she craned her head to look behind her.

Nothing.

Not trusting her eyes, Sabrina kept moving, although fatigue was finally slowing her down. She had a stitch in her side, and she couldn't seem to gulp enough oxygen as she ran to make it go away. Her arms and legs burned, and even her eyesight was blurring from exhaustion. And as if that weren't enough, her surroundings had taken on the golden hue that signified sunset less than an hour away.

At which point she'd be alone in the dark.

Ducking around a four-foot-wide giant sequoia, she pressed her back against its rough bark, hoping that he hadn't seen where she'd gone. Using the large evergreen for cover, she looked behind her at the trail of crushed grass and broken plants she'd made.

Nothing. Not even a sound.

She waited.

Still nothing. No noise, no movement, save the cry of some kind of eagle that was obviously nesting in the sequoia. She glanced up, but all she saw was the last of the daylight filtering through the canopy of pine boughs overhead. She turned back to the path.

She didn't know how long she stood there, frozen in place and waiting for her pursuer to come back out into the open. She knew she hadn't done enough to lose him—she'd just been trying to outrun him until she could figure out a plan. But maybe he'd given up on the steep pitch. Maybe he'd fallen and broken his damn neck.

She waited a little longer, scanning the ground around her until she spotted a thick but not-too-heavy-looking broken branch. Stepping out into the open, she snatched it up, brandishing it in front of her like a softball bat. It wasn't much, and he might even be able to grab it from her and use it to beat her over the head, but even still, she found the heavy weight of it comforting. Using the position of the sun as a guide, she oriented herself back southwest and headed once more for Mosley Gap.

She heard a rustling noise behind her, and she whirled around, clutching the branch.

Several yards away stood a young male deer, the fuzz not even off its stubby antlers. Its white tail shot up in warning and then it froze in place, staring at her. The large brown eyes didn't even blink.

"I know how you feel, dude." She turned back around.

And someone dropped down from the trees in front of her.

Sabrina screamed. She scuttled backward, watching him walk toward her, his dark eyes glinting behind the mask. Finally, her feet found their purchase, and she was about to pivot and take off running once more.

Oh, God. Ohgodohgodohgodohgod. It was all she could manage of a prayer as she raced through the forest, low-hanging boughs whipping across her arms and face.

She dropped the branch in favor of speed, pushed on by sheer terror.

She hadn't even heard him. She hadn't seen a thing. In spite of all her training.

It was almost too much. She wanted to stop, wanted to rest, curl up in a ball and just let him catch her so she could rest. So she could just face whatever he was, whatever he wanted.

She stumbled again. This time, there was no branch to save her.

Sabrina felt her feet leave the ground, her shin stinging from whatever she had hit. Time slowed enough for her to realize that it was going to hurt when she hit the ground. She stretched her arms out in front of her to absorb the hit she was about to take.

Her right knee crunched down on the ground first, followed by her hands. She cried out, and her arms buckled from the impact. She slid face first into a pile of leaves and branches, closing her eyes as bits of leaves and bark clung to her skin and found their way inside her mouth.

The scratches on her arms and face stinging like mad, Sabrina reached her hand out to steady herself, push herself up again. Try to get away from him one last time.

Her fingers brushed against something stiff but smooth, cool to the touch. She opened her eyes.

The first thing she noticed was a cluster of pale mountain dandelions, their sunny-yellow flowers closing slightly in the twilight. And then she saw it, still half-buried under the carefully constructed pile of natural debris that she'd fallen over.

A hand, its nails ragged and dirty, the waxy coating of death terrifyingly obvious.

"Jessie, oh, God," she whispered.

Chapter Nine

"Sabrina!"

At the sound of her name, Sabrina whirled around, expecting to see the man in the ski mask standing right before her. But he'd vanished, as if the whole thing had just been a terrible nightmare.

"Sabrina!"

Jessie. That was Jessie's voice. "Over here!" she shouted, scrambling to her feet, a lump of overwhelming gratitude lodged in her throat. A humming noise in the air made it difficult to figure out where her friend was coming from, but she was terrified that Jess would never make it.

Finally, Sabrina saw Jessie jogging toward her. And thankfully, no boogeymen snatched her away.

"Jess." She caught the tall blonde in her

arms, squeezing her thin frame tightly. "I thought you were—" She choked on the words, unable to complete that sentence.

"Sabrina, I'm so sorry. What happened?" The words came out in a rush as Jessie pulled back, still clutching Sabrina's elbows. "I had to make a pit stop, and when I came back you were gone. And that man's footprints—he chased you, didn't he?" She looked around wildly. "Where did he go? Did you lose him? Did you hear the chopper flying by? It might be in range, so we should try the radio."

"Of course." It hadn't even dawned on her that the humming sound she'd heard earlier might be the SAR helo. She tugged the radio from her belt and switched it on, her eyes drawn back to the mound at their feet. "Jess—"

Jessie's high-pitched gasp told her that she didn't have to say anything else. Dropping to her knees, Jessie started gently clearing the brush off the body. Sabrina assisted with her free hand as she used the other to bring the radio to her mouth.

"Air Watch RT64Z, Air Watch Romeo-Tango-six-four-Zulu, this is Tracking Team

One. Do you copy, over?" she said into
it, using the SAR helicopter's familiar
call sign.

A spectacular burst of static greeted
her when she lifted her thumb off the talk
button, and then she heard a garbled
answer that, while she couldn't understand
it, gave her a profound sense of relief. If the
speaker was Piper Watson—and she was
almost certain it was—the chopper pilot
would circle the area until the transmission
came in loud and clear.

Now they just had to wait. And hope that
when Piper did fly their way, she could find
a nearby place to land.

Clipping the radio back on her belt, she
bent down to help Jessie, who had uncovered a female torso from under the pile of
debris. Sabrina stepped over to where the
woman's face most likely was and concen-
trated her efforts there, brushing away the
leaves and dirt.

"Oh, she looks so young," Jessie murmured sadly.

She did look young, too young to have
had her life ended in such a brutal way.
Sabrina didn't know for sure, but her best
guess was that this was Jennifer Jenkins.

Her head was bent at an unnatural angle, her neck obviously broken. Her eyes were only partially opened, and her mouth was permanently frozen in a slack O of surprise. Jessie uncovered Jennifer's feet, checking out the soles of her boots. She gave a nod, letting Sabrina know that the shoes matched the tracks they'd been following.

She remembered Jennifer's boyfriend— the frantic worry and love and hope he'd conveyed when he'd stumbled out of the woods to tell them that he'd lost his girl. She reached out and swept a few bits of leaves off the woman's pale cheek, ran her fingers down the eyelids to close them all the way.

Another family whose hearts would be broken tonight. "I'm sorry, Jennifer," she whispered.

The chopping whir of an approaching helicopter interrupted her thoughts.

"Tracking Team One, this is Air Watch RT64Z. Do you copy, over?"

Sabrina snatched up her radio. "Air Watch, this is Tracking Team One." She looked up to see the silver underside of the helo pass directly overhead. "We're right underneath you, Piper. Requesting pickup as soon as you are able to land, over."

"Base has been trying to reach you. Do you have any messages to relay, over?"

Sabrina glanced at the body on the ground. "Tell them to get as many police personnel out here as possible," she said. "We've got a body to carry out, Air Watch, over."

"That's affirmative. Relaying message," came the reply. There was a pause, and then the pilot came back on the radio. Sabrina could hear the chopper circling back toward them. "There's a clearing less than a click south of the area I just passed over," Piper said. "Just follow my lead, ladies, and I'll take you home."

SABRINA AND Jessie followed the sound of the helicopter to the clearing, relief an almost palpable thing between them. And when Aaron stepped out, rifle in hand, and started walking toward her, Sabrina felt something lift inside her, at last feeling as though the danger was past—for now. She broke into a fast walk, and then a run, and before she realized what she was doing and in front of whom, she'd thrown her arms around his neck and was holding on as tightly as she could.

He put the arm that wasn't holding his gun around her waist and just held her while Piper shut down the helicopter. She couldn't control her shaking, so she just clung to him.

"Sabrina," he murmured into her ear as the chopper blades behind them slowed and the engine hummed to a stop. "What's going on?"

"He was here. He followed Jennifer Jenkins, a woman who'd been out here camping with her boyfriend. God, I think he stalked her." The words just came flooding out, and she couldn't stop them. "He killed her, Aaron. We found the body. I don't think you should see—"

"Show me."

His entire body stiffened, and she could see that he was shutting down again, the icy demeanor she'd grown so accustomed to firmly back in place. But she was starting to see that for what it was—a coping mechanism. And the thought of Aaron trying to cope with seeing a dead woman close to his daughter's age made her ache for him.

"Aaron—"

He softened, just a bit. "It's okay. Just show me."

They walked back to the body, Aaron holding his gun at the ready. His face was unreadable as he looked down at the young woman, lying half-buried in the leaves. He crouched down, his fingers automatically feeling for a pulse. Sabrina looked away, telling herself it was so she could keep an eye out for danger, knowing that wasn't the full reason.

Aaron ran his fingers along her neck, the rest of him so still, she turned back and waited to see what he'd do, if he'd need her somehow.

"Her neck is broken. The medical examiner can tell us more, but it feels like a clean snap." He let his hand fall away from Jennifer's body. "That's something we learn in the military special forces— how to break someone's neck with your bare hands, in one blow."

"Do you think—?"

He shrugged. "Maybe. Maybe not. But now we know he's strong. You found out that he's fast."

And then, the remote, detached police detective was gone, and in his place was the father. "Sabrina, I've always believed she was out there." Aaron's eyes went wild, and he scrubbed a hand across his face, vibrating with pent-up energy and with a deep, cold fear. "What if I'm wrong? What if she's gone?"

She didn't know what to say to that, so she just took his hand and held it. "Aaron, if that's not the case, you're all she's got. Don't give up hope now. Not until we find her." And she hoped, so much, that that was a promise she could keep.

GOD WAS DEAD, but the Overman couldn't help but feel godlike at the thought of his ability to outsmart everything the "authorities"—the word made him laugh— threw at him as he added to his ranks. And someday soon, all of his hard work would be rewarded.

A race of Overmen.

For now, he was the only one. And today he would celebrate that, revel in what he was.

Wrapping his hand around the crude mortal's slim, white neck, feeling it convulse as it gasped for air, as the arteries in its eyes exploded a brilliant red. Watching the last bits of its pathetic life drain from its body.

If there had been a God, that would be what he felt like.

He hadn't intended to take its life, but it struggled, it hurt him, just like his latest conquest had hurt him. He might have to do the same to her, just to show the others what he could do if they refused to accept the gift he was giving them. And then he'd bring the one called Sabrina, the strong one, the one who had already transcended some physical limitations. She might be worthy. She might see where these beasts did not.

He paced back and forth, watching them in silence, while they shivered and whimpered, poor, pathetic beasts. The one who had tried to escape sagged against her chains, her head bowed, a crude, limited being at last aware of her limitations.

She was "it" to him now. They all were, and so they would remain, until they grew over and above themselves and took a new name after they'd ascended. Overman. A race of Overmen.

When he felt they were ready, he spoke, quoting the philosopher, the great Nietzsche: "The awakening of moral observation has become necessary."

He picked up the knife that had been

resting on the small table near the door, one he'd brought down to their hovel just for this occasion. It had hurt him, and it needed to be punished. The others needed to see what he could do.

"Mankind can no longer be spared the cruel sight of the moral dissecting table and its knives," he continued. Brandishing the knife before his face so they could see, he feasted his eyes on the one who had gone from student to prey.

"Mankind is something that must be overcome."

He froze, the knife falling from his grasp, and he threw his head back, giving himself over to the laughter bubbling up inside him. His entire body starting to sing in ecstasy at the words one of them had finally dared to speak.

"I'm dissatisfied with myself," the voice continued, a hint of desperation in its tone. It was like that, the first time you could really see. "I choose to be better than I am."

He opened his eyes, walked to the one who had finally risen above herself. "Rosie," he said lovingly, stroking her dirty face. She was his. She'd come home. All of his careful, hard work, everything he'd been had been for the creation of this moment.

"Tell me, master, how shall I overcome Man?" Her voice was small, shaking, but the resolve in her eyes was fierce. Such was the burning of the new evolution.

"Tell me how to evolve like you did," she said.

He unfastened her chains, taking her by the hand and leading her into the light, the unenlightened in his audience all but forgotten. Let them learn from this moment. Let them see.

"I'll show you," he said.

Chapter Ten

Aaron pulled his car up to her house, and she just sat, looking young and vulnerable and more lost and alone than he'd ever seen her. When they'd gotten back to the ranger station, he's insisted on having an EMT check her out. She was pretty banged up, but other than a large cut on her forehead—which the EMT had covered with a butterfly bandage after Sabrina had refused to have a doctor look at it—she was fine. A fact of which she'd consistently reminded him as he drove her home. But now, all of the fire seemed to have left her as the trauma of a very exhausting, very long day set in.

"Sabrina." He paused, cleared his throat while staring straight ahead at her garage door. "I don't think you should be alone tonight. If he knows who you are, he might be watching." He turned, looked at her, trying to anticipate how he'd counter her inevitable protest. "I thought I'd stay, if you don't mind."

"Okay."

Okay? Now he was really starting to worry. She got out of the car, and he followed, coming inside her house after her.

"You can stay in the guest bedroom," she said. "I'll get you a new set of sheets. I haven't changed them since my brother slept there." She gave him a small smile and headed upstairs. He wasn't sure whether he should follow her or not, but he did anyway.

She rummaged through a small linen closet at the top of the stairs, pulling out a set of pale green bedsheets with pink flowers on them and handing them to him as she guided him into a small room that served as an office, he guessed, since there was a computer on a desk in the corner. Next to it, a futon was folded into its sofa position. He noticed she wouldn't meet his eyes.

"Sabrina?"

"Hmmm?"

He took the sheets from her and set them

down on a nearby chest of drawers. "It's not your fault."

Her dark eyebrows drew together. "I'm not—"

"Rosie, Tara, Jennifer. None of this is your fault. That's why you're not looking at me, isn't it?"

She shook her head, but she still wasn't meeting his eyes. "No. I'm fine."

He took her gently by the shoulders. "It's not your fault. God, I've never seen someone work so hard. You did everything you could for those girls."

Swallowing, she reached up and rested a palm on his chest, looking as though she would push him away, then just touching him. Her mouth quivered, but she didn't say anything.

He bent his knees to dip down to her level, brushing her chin with his fingertips, and finally, she did meet his gaze. Her pale, golden eyes were filled with guilt, when he was the one who should—and did—feel guilty. "I should never, never have blamed you. I'm sorry, Sabrina. I've never been more sorry in my life."

She gave him a little frown, a look so vulnerable, something inside his chest ached, but she didn't cry. "I have no idea what it's like to lose a daughter, but I see the way my sister is with her kids. It must consume you. And to have everyone cut off the last bit of your hope like I did…" She trailed off, shaking her head.

"He did that," Aaron countered. "The man who took her and didn't leave us any more clues. You had nothing to do with this. You would have found her if she could have been found."

She bowed her head. "I hope so. I always wonder if I missed something, those first few days of the search."

"If you missed it, I did, too." He fingered a tendril of her hair that had come loose at her temple. "We all did. Sabrina, you're one of the best people I know. No matter what happens in the end, Rosie and I have been lucky to have you looking for her."

Without thinking, he leaned over and brought his mouth to hers.

SHE COULDN'T believe it. After everything they'd been through, all her guilt, all his pain, they'd ended up in her home, in each other's arms. His kiss was soft, gentle, but she could sense the pent-up emotion behind it that he kept hidden behind his grief.

"Sabrina, I can't—" he began. She froze, aching at the thought of letting him go now. Not now.

Taking a deep breath, she stepped back, prepared to do the grown-up thing if she had to. But she knew that Aaron needed her as much as she needed him. Maybe more, in a way. Maybe all she represented was a way to push the images of Jennifer out of his mind, to keep thoughts of his daughter's suffering at bay.

It was too heavy a burden to put on one man. Too much for him to carry, and as she got her desire under control, she knew she wanted just to lift it from him, just for a little while.

"Aaron," she murmured, cupping his rough cheek with her hand. He closed his eyes, leaned into her touch. "Let go. Please. I think you need to, just for a moment." She stood on her tiptoes, brushing his mouth softly with hers.

A single tear slipped down one cheek, and she thought that she'd never seen him cry, for all that he'd been through. She wondered if he ever had, or if he'd just kept all that emotion and worry and heartache buried far from the surface, masking it with constant action.

"We can forget it ever happened tomorrow, Aaron, but I just want you to let me take some of this from you for a few hours." She moved one hand off his face, trailing it down the side of his neck and onto the flat planes of his chest. She let her hand rest there, a silent invitation, waiting to see if he'd make the next move. "I want you." She swallowed. "So much. Forget it all for one night, and look at me."

He opened his eyes then, and they shone silver in the soft light from her desk lamp. "I'm looking at you, Sabrina," he said softly. She tilted her head up, and he brought his mouth to hers.

His kiss was soft, at first, nibbling, tasting, seeing how much she wanted, how much he needed to hold back.

Sabrina threaded her fingers into the hair curling slightly at his nape, pulling him closer. "Aaron," she whispered, pleading for something she couldn't voice. His hands ran along her back, up and down her arms, touching her in places that shouldn't thrill her this much, but they did.

She slipped her own hands underneath the hem of his T-shirt, her fingers brushing against the taut skin over his stomach.

"I need you, Sabrina," he whispered into her mouth.

She tugged upward, until she'd pulled his shirt up as far as it would go. He stepped back and shucked it in one graceful movement, taking her breath away. As soon as he'd tossed it to the side, she had her hands on him again, one trailing up the indentation near his spine, the other moving across his chest, up to his shoulders, pulling his head down to hers once more. She put everything she felt, everything she wanted into the kiss she gave him then. "Yes," she said.

With a growl of satisfaction, he cupped her rear with his hands, lifting her up until she wrapped her legs around his waist and could feel just how much he wanted her. She tangled both hands in his hair, her breath coming in ragged gasps, and somewhere in the back of her mind, she knew they wouldn't make it to her bed this time. What was between them was just too powerful for niceties like that.

He turned and pinned her back against the wall, his hand moving under her shirt, undoing the front clasp of her bra. She didn't know how she managed it, but she peeled off her shirt with one hand, throwing it on the floor as her bra fell open. And then his tongue was in her mouth and he was pressing against her, and his bare, masculine skin felt so incredible against hers, she thought she'd die from it.

He moved his mouth down the side of her jaw, down her neck, sending chills down her body. And then lower still, until he captured her nipple in his warm, wet mouth, and she cried out, bowing her head against the top of his, her hands tangled once more in his soft hair.

Just when she thought she'd lose it completely, he rose and kissed her way too softly for her taste. "Bed?"

"Hmmm?" she murmured, kissing him harder. They both lost themselves in each other for a moment, and then he pulled back.

"Where's your bed?"

She tightened her legs around him and rocked, eliciting a soft moan from him. "Shut up, Aaron, I don't need a bed," she murmured.

He laughed softly, and her heart thrilled at

the sound. He turned toward her desk, pressed her against it, sweeping the few books and papers on it to the ground. She let go of him, her skin feeling exposed and bare now that it wasn't pressed against him, and lay back, allowing him to slip her pants and underwear down her hips and off her legs.

"Sabrina, you're so beautiful," he murmured, his eyes traveling up and down her body. His hands went to his fly, and she sat up, stopping him with her own hands.

"Let me," she said. She undid his zipper in one swift movement, brushing against him with her hand and loving the sound he made deep in his throat. She pushed his pants down over his lean hips, kicking them the rest of the way with her heel, and then, oh, yes, then he was inside her, moving against her, laying her back against the cool wood of the desk and devouring her neck and her mouth with his lips. She wrapped her legs around him and drove him in deeper, deeper, deeper still, until everything she felt and everything she wanted grew too big to contain, and she cried out, rocking against him.

He collapsed onto her, whispering her name, and she stroked his back, loving this moment afterward. Too soon, he raised himself up on his elbows, looking down at her with so much emotion in his gray eyes. "Sabrina," he murmured. "Tell me where your bed is, because next time, I'm going to do this right."

She bit her lip and smiled, then touched his cheek and told him, and he carried her to her room. As they made love again, slowly and gently, taking their time and savoring each other, she knew that she'd fallen for him. But she also knew that he'd never be hers, because one night, as astonishing as it was, would never be able to erase the hole in his heart.

SOMETIME in the middle of the night, Sabrina awoke as Aaron thrashed in bed next to her, in the grip of the worst kind of nightmare.

"Rosie. No, God, not you. Please." His voice broke, and he slammed his arm against the mattress, pushing away something only he could see.

"Aaron." She turned, trying to wrap her arms around him.

He turned, moaning softly, still asleep but seeing way too much.

"Shh." She ran her palm against his back, up and down his arm, a soft, trailing movement meant to soothe. His breath caught, and he murmured something unintelligible. She shushed him again.

"Sabrina," he sighed, and she moved closer, spooning against his back and wrapping one arm around his waist. She blew a cooling breath on the back of his neck, damp from a panicked, dreaming sweat.

"I have to find her." He tensed again, and she could see in the pale moonlight that streamed through the sheer curtains at her bedroom window that his eyes were still closed.

"I promise you, I'll do everything I can to find her." She rubbed his back, blowing on his neck again until his body stilled. "Shh. Sleep now."

She held and shushed and soothed him until his sleep was quiet again. And she wondered whether it would ever be possible to soothe Aaron's nightmares for good.

SEVERAL HOURS later, Sabrina was startled awake when Aaron abruptly sat up in bed, the bedsheet pooling around his waist.

"Go back to sleep," she murmured,

batting at him in an ineffectual attempt to get him to lie back down.

"Sabrina, someone's in your house."

That woke her up, and she, too, shot up in bed, clutching the sheet over her chest and listening for whatever it was that he'd heard. It wasn't hard—a trio of male voices and pounding, busybody feet made their way up the stairs, coming at her door much too quickly.

"Aaron, it's my—" she began, but the door swung open before she could explain.

"Hey, surprise, peanut. We— Oh, crap." Patricio spun around and exited the room as quickly as he'd entered it, nearly knocking her other brother Joe down in his haste to leave.

"What the heck, Rico? You nearly made me spill her coff—" Joe looked up and froze completely when he saw her, holding a steaming mug in front of him. He looked at her, then at Aaron, then back to her again, and his expression darkened. "You know this guy, Sabrina?"

She sighed, trying to hide her utter mortification behind a veneer of exasperation. "No, Joe, I just picked him up off the street and asked if he'd like to have a go at it. What do you think?"

Patricio's twin Danny entered, shielding his eyes with his hand. "Uh, Joe, what do you say we give our little sister some privacy? Like I recommended before you two went charging up here like a couple of mad cows."

"She likes her coffee in the morning," Joe muttered, turning around.

Patricio reached in and gripped Joe's arm, yanking him out the door. "Apparently there's someone she likes even more in the morning. Get outta there, you idiot."

"Uh, sorry Bree." Still covering his eyes, Danny turned to follow. "Mind if we wait downstairs?"

Sabrina gave a choked laugh as he closed the door. "No. No, go ahead," she said loudly, to make sure he heard her in his haste to depart.

"Take your time!" Patricio called from the stairwell, and for some odd reason, that was the statement that finally made her blush. She sneaked a look at Aaron, who was leaning calmly against her headboard, looking completely at ease with himself.

"What? Tell me you didn't find that completely and utterly mortifying?"

He smiled at her, and she realized it was the first time she'd ever seen him look so carefree. "Being caught in bed with a gorgeous woman? Not at all. I'm feeling kinda proud of myself at the moment."

She laughed and swiped at him with her pillow.

"They're not going to try and hurt me, are they?"

"No, but I might just hurt them." She wrapped the sheet tighter around her body, hoping she didn't die of embarrassment when she finally confronted them. "I mean, that's so not the way I imagined this morning would be."

His eyes sparkled at her words. "So, what did you imagine?"

She grinned. "I'm not sure you're man enough to handle what I imagined, Donovan."

He reached out, pulled her to him, and her breath caught as their bodies came into contact once more. "I think I just might be." He leaned down and kissed her softly.

"Mmmm." She lost herself in him for a moment, then remembered that her brothers were directly below them. "I should go see what's up with the Three Stooges." She pulled away reluctantly. "I'll shower quick, and then you can have it."

"Sure." He lifted his hand, stroked her cheek with his thumb. "You're beautiful in the morning."

The smile she gave him was private, intimate, and they just looked at each other until a series of shouts interrupted the moment. Laughing, she pulled away. "I'd better get down there before they kill each other." She got off the bed, then turned to him again, suddenly. "Don't go." She knew the dream between them had to end, and soon, but she couldn't let it go just yet.

"I won't," he said softly.

She showered and headed downstairs, where her brothers were all congregated in her kitchen.

Daniel, the one with the closest thing to a sense of propriety, shoved his hand through his short hair. "Sabrina, we're really sorry."

"I believe I told you we should call first," Patricio piped up.

"Look, it's okay. It doesn't matter." She waved them off, feeling a strange combination of mortification and irritation, yet loving them all the same. "What are you all doing here? Rico, I thought you were going back to L.A. today?"

"Yeah, well." He handed her a mug filled with coffee. A lump of uneven milk foam floated sadly at the top—they'd obviously tried to make her a latte, and had failed miserably. "I heard about what happened yesterday afternoon."

"And he told us," Joe interjected.

"So we thought we'd see if you needed us," Daniel finished. "We wanted to make sure you were okay. We all took some leave, if you want us to stay here with you until they catch this guy."

"We could go up on the trails with you," Joe said after downing a small glass of orange juice. "We can't track anything, but we look scary."

The three of them nodded their heads and waited.

Shaking her head, she reached for the one nearest her—Patricio—and hugged him tightly. "How do you find this stuff out? Even the media doesn't know yet."

"I—"

"—have your ways. I know," she finished for him. She hugged Joe and Danny in turn, truly appreciating that they cared about her enough to drop everything the way they had. "I'll be okay. Aaron is… He doesn't have anyone at home right now. I think I can get him to stay with me, and he's been coming up with Alex and Jessie and me when we're working."

"Yeah, but what good is he? Small-town cop compared to P.I. of the year—" Patricio pointed at Joe "—a member of the LAPD's elite homicide squad—" he indicated Danny "—and me?"

"Captain Dangerous himself?" Danny finished. Patricio cuffed him in the back of the head, which degenerated for a moment into them trading a series of head slaps until each was satisfied. They were all perfect grown-ups, she'd noticed, until you got all three of them in one room, and then things just went south. In a completely adorable way.

"Trust me. I'll have plenty of protection." She turned to Joe. "You left Emma alone at home with a toddler?" And then she addressed Danny. "And isn't it your anniversary soon? And Rico, I know you don't want to leave your wife when she's pregnant." She made a shooing motion.

"Go home, you guys. I love you, and I appreciate this so much, but I'll be fine. We know what we're dealing with now, and we're not going to take any risks."

"You sure?" Joe folded his arms, looking skeptical.

She nodded. "I'm sure."

"Ours is not to smother. We're outta here. We only had Sadie's private plane for the day, anyway, and then we were going to have to fly coach. Rico hates coach," Joe said. Patricio's wife Sadie was an A-list movie and TV star, so she generously provided all sorts of perks to the rest of the family, including her private plane for times when they all wanted to be together.

Sabrina hugged them again and walked them to the door. "Better go, then."

"Bree, we mean it. If you need us, just call, and we can be here in hours. With the wives' blessings," Danny said as they walked out the door. Then they got into a shiny, red sports car that Joe had obviously picked out, and drove off. It was only then that she realized they hadn't said a word about Aaron.

As if he'd read her thoughts, he came

downstairs, showered and dressed and obviously ready to go.

"Morning," he said, his smile a little bit shy.

"Morning." She hung back, knowing everything was about to go back to how it had been before and wanting time to stop all the same.

And then he reached for her, and she was in his arms, clinging to him tightly and not wanting to let him go.

"Sabrina—" He ran his hand along her back, searching for the right words. "I just wanted to tell you, that if I don't call... Last night was amazing. I just— You deserve more than this. I feel...lost. Missing my daughter...it kills me, every day, and I won't take you there with me."

"What if you find her?" She didn't have to say who she meant. "What happens then?"

She felt him bow his head into her hair. "Then I'll show up at your doorstep and beg you to marry me," he said softly.

Her breath caught, and she closed her eyes and let herself lean into him, just for a minute longer. It was a beautiful dream.

He straightened, and she knew he was going to pull away. She reached out, cupping his cheek with her hand, looking him in the eye because she wanted him to know how much she meant what she was going to say.

"I love you. I know it's too soon, and I know the circumstances aren't right, and I know I'm supposed to wait until you say it first, but I do." Tears welled up in her eyes, and for the first time in her life, she didn't care that someone could see them. "I just wanted you to know…" She paused, swallowing as she tried to bring herself under control. "I'm here. Always."

He laid his hand on top of hers. "You give me peace, Sabrina," he said. Then he leaned forward and brushed his lips against her cheek, stepped back and let her go.

Chapter Eleven

When Sabrina reported for her shift at the ranger station that day, Aaron was outside waiting for her. Along with about twenty reporters. She blinked in surprise when a woman in a dark blue suit shoved her fist, which was wrapped around a small digital voice recorder, into her face.

"Ms. Adelante, Pam Hartman, *Port Renegade Tribune-Herald,*" the woman said by way of introduction, her words coming out like a rapid-fire hail of bullets. She glanced around at Pam's colleagues, who, unlike Pam, obviously didn't think Sabrina was of any significance. "What can you tell us about the dead woman your team found yesterday?"

"Uhhh." How the heck did the press know about it already? As far as she knew, the police hadn't finished notifying Jennifer Jenkins's family yet. She glanced over the small crowd at Aaron, who was leaning against a wall, his eyes hooded as he ignored the people shouting around him. He gave a nearly imperceptible shake of his head at her. "No comment?"

"Is the body you found yesterday in any way connected with Tara Fisher's disappearance?" the woman continued, matching her stride for stride.

"I have no idea." She quickened her pace, making Pam jog in her sensible brown shoes to keep up.

"Is any of this in any way connected to Rosie Donovan's disappearance six months ago?"

"You'd have to ask the police that. We just find lost hikers." Keeping her focus on the station doors, she kept walking, the reporter dogging her heels like her conscience personified.

"Is it true that the kidnapper left you a message personally?"

"What?" She skidded to a halt on the gravel and could only stare at the reporter. "Where the heck did you—? No comment!" If he had, there was no way the *Tribune-*

Herald would have known about it first, was there?

Then again, she had been a little preoccupied last night. She looked at Aaron again. He was still watching her from his perch on the ranger station's porch. The other reporters, sensing her agitation like a school of sharks reacting to blood in the water, looked as though they were taking a newfound interest in who she was and what she might know. Several were making their way toward her.

"Ms. Adelante, I know I look like a pesky hack to you, but I'm trying to protect the women in our community." Pam's expression had grown softer, her voice losing its aggressive tone. "Is there anything I can tell them?"

Sabrina's shoulders slumped at the question. She'd been so busy trying to find the missing women that she hadn't given much thought to those who were still potential victims, who could still be protected. Granted, that was Skylar's job, but still…

Skylar was going to kill her. But honestly, she didn't care.

"Tell them to keep out of the park," she

said, avoiding Aaron's gaze. "Tell them to drive south, or head for the coast if they want to go hiking, but they should keep out of the park here. Or, at the very least, only hike in large parties. It's not safe to go alone."

"Why isn't it safe?"

Sabrina shook her head. "Skylar or the police department can give you the particulars." *They'd better.* "But what I can tell you is that there's someone very dangerous on the trails right now, and he's targeting young women. Tell them to be careful."

With that, she pushed through the glass double doors. It wasn't as though the ranger station had security, so she wondered why Pam didn't follow her and continue pushing for answers.

Until she saw the horde of police detectives and patrol officers milling about the main room, which was set up for tourists and hikers, with display cases, photographs and a couple of metal turnstiles with hiking and area maps. Aaron came inside a few seconds after she did, and he moved in behind her, his fingertips on her elbow with a sweet intimacy that made her want to cry.

"Hey," she said softly.

"Hey. We've been waiting for you."

She craned her neck to shoot him a look that she hoped conveyed her puzzlement. But before he could explain further, Skylar moved into her line of sight.

"Oh, good, Sabrina's here." She turned in a half circle and addressed the growing crowd of law- enforcement and SAR trackers around her. "If we could all move into the briefing room, please." She didn't have to say it more than once before people started moving. "Bree, can you step into my office, please?"

"Sure." She followed Skylar inside, Aaron close behind. She thought they would close the door, but then Eddie Ventaglia stepped inside, too, as well as Alex and Jessie.

"Alex, how are you feeling?" she asked. He still looked a bit pale, but otherwise seemed a lot better than he'd been twenty-four hours earlier.

Alex grimaced. "Fine. I'm sorry, Bree. If I hadn't been ralphing all over the place, you know I would've been on that mountain with you and Jess yesterday."

"Thank you for that lovely visual," Jessie said, then patted his arm in a reassuring manner.

Ventaglia cleared his throat, and the three of them turned to give him their full attention.

"Ms. Adelante, I'm not going to beat around the bush here. There's been a message."

She looked down at the piece of paper he held in his hands, a Xerox copy of a handwritten note on much smaller paper, the area around the edges dark gray. "A message? From Jennifer's killer?"

Ventaglia nodded, leaning back to perch his right hip on Skylar's oak desk. He tapped his fingertips on the back of the paper, creating a loud rustling sound.

Confused, she folded her arms, dread pooling in her stomach at the thought of where this conversation was going. "Detective, why did you address me directly? What does this have to do with me?"

"The note was addressed to you, Sabrina," Aaron cut in.

Oh, God. Not only was a killer out there in the state park, but now he was communicating directly with her? What was next, letters from prison? She reached her hand out. "Let me see."

Taking the note from Ventaglia, she was horrified to see the words, To Sabrina Adelante, written carefully across the top. He printed, rather than wrote in cursive, and all of his letters were perfectly uniform, the lines of text showing evidence that he'd used a ruler to keep them straight and evenly spaced.

If all goes well, the time will come when one will take up this letter rather than the Bible as a guide to morals and reason. We are more than beast, more than Man. Your skill shows you have true potential, your skills are un-matched in the land of beasts, but will you ever overcome what you are? Free will is insignificant—what matters is the will to power.

She skimmed the next few lines, which were just some crazy blah-blah-blah about transcending the "insignificant morality of Man" and the next step in human evolution.

He'd put the last two lines in boldface, and she figured they were what was really important.

> Start from the beginning, at the sign of the Rose, and follow. I am willing to teach you if you are up to the challenge.
> She is free when she is with herself. Come *alone,* and you may find her.
> Overman

"Overman?" She dropped her hand so the paper rustled against her thigh. "What does that mean?"

"Nietzsche," Jessie muttered, looking most definitely creeped out as she read over Sabrina's shoulder.

"Also known as the *Übermensch.* It's Nietzsche's concept of the next step on the evolutionary ladder," Alex interjected, waving his hands around as he explained. "He believed that you had to be dissatisfied with yourself and work to overcome your base humanity to achieve something greater. Artists, philosophers, saints were becoming Overmen, but people have been arguing since he posited the theory what an actual Overman would be like."

They all stared at him.

"What?" He shrugged, folding his arms. "I was a philosophy minor in school. Have to have something to think about when you're staring at the ground all day," he grumbled.

"Wow. That was unexpected." Sabrina brought the note over to Aaron, her arm brushing his as she pointed to the last few lines to draw his attention to them. "But look at this part at the end. Is he seriously challenging me? It sounds like he wants me to track him."

"That's how we interpreted it, too," Ventaglia responded.

"And this sentence: 'She is free when she is with herself.' Who's the 'she'?"

Aaron caught her gaze and held it, and she nearly felt her heart break at the hope she saw in his expression. She knew without a doubt who he thought "she" might be.

"Can't say," Aaron replied softly. "But yes, he's challenging you."

"That letter is just a bastardization of Nietzsche's quotes. It's like the Nazis, perverting his work to justify their whole 'master race' idea. The Overman had his own moral code. This guy is using

Nietzsche to justify taking these girls," Alex said behind them.

"What. Ever." As always, action triumphed over words for Sabrina, and she picked up her backpack, slinging it over her shoulders. The nut who called himself the Overman had thrown down a gauntlet, and she wasn't about to waste daylight thinking about it—she meant to answer the challenge, and answer it now.

"Let's go." She headed for the door.

"Wait—" Ventaglia began.

"Go where, Sabrina?" Jessie interrupted, her words stopping Sabrina. "Just where do you think you're going to start?"

"He told us. He said to start at the beginning, at the sign of the Rose."

"Don't tell me you speak Whackjob," Alex interjected, his dark eyebrows drawn together in puzzlement. "Where is the beginning? What the hell is the sign of the Rose?"

Sabrina bounced on the balls of her feet, itching to hit the road. She might have avoided any and all philosophy classes in college, but it wasn't like the Overman was a master of cryptology or anything. "The beginning is where Rosie Donovan disappeared, where we were following her sign. Get it?" She splayed her hands and widened her eyes at Alex, giving him a second to process what she'd just told him. "Rosie was his first victim, that we know of, and the first time we started trailing him. Since he's communicating directly with me, that's our beginning."

She stole a glance at Aaron. He didn't confirm her assertion, but his eyes were bright, and the pent-up energy coming off him was explosive. Like her, he just wanted to move.

"That was my theory, too," he said, looking at Ventaglia. Then he addressed her directly. "But we can't let you go up there."

"Right. So you're just going to spoil the best and, may I add, only lead you've had in months? Come on, Aaron, don't get all soft about my safety. Jess? Alex? You coming?" she threw over her shoulder. The two didn't answer, instead preferring just to gather their things.

"Ms. Adelante, no one is going up there who's not Port Renegade PD," Ventaglia boomed, his voice practically dripping with authority. "This is a dangerous man we're dealing with."

"Last I heard, state park rangers are considered law enforcement. And as law enforcement, Skylar can deploy her trackers anywhere she likes, and you have no jurisdiction." She looked expectantly at Skylar, who had been standing on the outside of their little group, quietly taking in the conversation.

Skylar surprised her by shaking her head. "Bree, I can't let you put yourself in danger like that. He said to come alone. You can't go up against a killer by yourself."

"Sky, what else are we going to do?" She whirled around to confront Aaron. "This is your daughter he's referring to. What if my going up there helps you find her?"

"What if it gets you killed?" he countered softly. "Sabrina, our medical examiner took one look at Jennifer Jenkins's body yesterday and confirmed that he'd probably broken her neck with one quick snap of his hands. This is not someone I'd ever send a twenty-six-year-old woman up against."

"Then what are you going to do?" she asked, looking from Aaron to Eddie Ventaglia.

"We'll disguise one of our officers to

look as much like you as possible. We'll plant SWAT and undercover officers on the trails and hope we can catch him before he eludes us again," the big detective replied.

She had to admit, the plan sounded impressive, but on the whole, it was just impractical, and she had to make them see that. "He implies in this note that he's going to be setting a trail. Do you have anyone in your department with any tracking abilities whatsoever?"

"Field and Weiss."

Sabrina snorted. "Whom I trained. In two hours, so they would know enough to stay out of my way when I helped you find that prison escapee near Lake Crescent." She pointed outside, as if she even cared what direction the faraway lake was in. "I'm a journeyman-level tracker, and Alex and Jessie are close to that level. Do you have any idea how many hours we've put in reading sign on the ground to do what we do? Sending Field or Weiss, as capable as they are, is like playing darts with a blind person, and both of you know that."

Aaron sighed. "Sabrina, you're putting yourself and your team in danger."

"My team, Aaron, can't come with me. The note says I'm supposed to go alone."

"Then you're putting yourself in danger."

She rubbed the bridge of her nose, tired of arguing while the minutes ticked by. "And you didn't when you joined the military? There are two girls—maybe more—out there who need to come home. I can do this."

Skylar fiddled with the bow of her glasses. "I told you two she wouldn't stand for this."

Ventaglia nodded. "You did."

"So that's the plan then." She knew she was being presumptuous, but maybe it would get the detectives to move that much faster.

"You're wearing Kevlar," Aaron said. "I don't care how heavy or hot it is, or how much faster you think you can go without it. You're wearing it."

She nodded. "Okay."

"You'll wear an earpiece, be in contact with law enforcement at all times. Like Eddie said, there'll be undercover officers posing as hikers throughout the park. They'll be around to assist you."

The thought made her feel a little more

secure. Now that they were actually going forward with the plans, she couldn't help but feel a little nervous at the thought of coming face-to-face with the so-called Overman.

"And I'm going up with you," Aaron said.

She narrowed her eyes. "But the note said I'm supposed to come alone. You don't think he'll see you and run?"

"He won't see me." With that, he walked out of the room.

She didn't know how he was going to pull that one off. The Overman knew who she was, which meant that he likely had been stalking her team and had an excellent idea of what Aaron looked like. But whether Aaron was somehow going to shadow her without being seen or walk beside her wearing a plastic moustache and glasses, it didn't matter. All that mattered was that they get going.

"Okay. Then let's move."

SABRINA WAITED for Aaron inside the station for a few minutes, but then she suddenly just needed to get outside, fast. Pushing through the double doors, she headed for her Jeep, parked at the far edge of the lot, next to the forest line. A stand of young Douglas firs shaded her car from the morning sunlight, the ground beneath them a snarl of lady ferns, spike moss and a sprinkling of tiny yellow wood sorrel blooms.

"Bree, wait!" Alex called after her.

"Are you going to be okay?" Looking paler than usual, Jessie gnawed on her thumbnail as she and Alex closed the gap between them and Sabrina. "I hate the idea of you going up there without us."

"I'm fine." She had to smile at Jessie's concern. "Don't worry—this is what they pay us the big bucks for."

Alex snorted at the reference to their park employee salary, which pretty much hovered around the "measly" level, even for those trackers with lots of seniority built up. "Where'd Donovan go?" he asked. "He's still going up with you, right?"

"He is, if he ever stops primping and gets out here." She opened the door to her Jeep and threw her backpack inside, ready to drive up to the Dungeness Falls trailhead as soon as Aaron showed himself. "I don't know where he went."

"Not to go primp, that's for sure," one of

the trees said in Aaron's deep baritone, making them all jump. Sabrina squinted at the trees, but she couldn't see any sign of human life in there.

"Uh, Aaron? Where are you?"

"Here." A thick, brushy patch of spike moss that she'd thought was growing on a pile of sticks and other forest detritus detached itself from one of the trees and rose upward. The detritus followed suit, and that's when she realized the whole mess was slightly Aaron-shaped. When two gray eyes peered out at her, the whites around the pupils standing out in startling clarity, she knew it was, indeed, Aaron. Wearing one impressive-as-all-get-out disguise.

Stepping forward, she fingered a bit of his costume, which, upon seriously close inspection revealed itself to be a thick, furry weave of burlap pieces, cut into grasslike strips in some places and twisted to look like small twigs in others. He'd smeared green camouflage paint over his face and had covered himself from head to toe in the burlap, even tying pieces around his rifle. Crouching down and covering his face, as he had been, he was pretty much invisible. And though he was now standing up, he still had a disconcerting air of being half man, half topiary about him.

"Holy crap, you're like a ninja," Alex said, clearly impressed. "If one of its parents had mated with the shrubbery."

Sabrina squinted at Aaron's "outfit," for lack of a better word, stroking her chin with exaggerated thoughtfulness. "Actually, I thought he looked more like the Snuffle-upagus. You know, from *Sesame Street*. Except moldy."

"Yes!" Alex whirled on her, clearly having a moment. "Remember that episode where he and Big Bird went to Hawaii and there was a Snuffleupagus-shaped mountain?"

Aaron calmly adjusted the burlap sleeve on his rifle, then hit the ground and flattened in the shallow ditch between the Jeep and the trees. The freaky thing about that was that even though she knew where he was, she still couldn't distinguish him from the rest of the undergrowth around him.

"I don't know about you guys," Jessie said, staring at the ground. "But I think the weird suit is kind of impressive."

"I'll agree to that," Sabrina said.

"I just wanted you to know, just because you don't see me doesn't mean I'm not there," Aaron said. "Get to the trailhead. I'll be within earshot, every step of the way." Then he edged back and melted into the woods.

"It's called a ghillie suit," Alex supplied helpfully as they stared at the spot where Aaron had been, each undoubtedly trying to catch a glimpse of him, which was proving impossible. "Military snipers wear them while stalking people they want to snipe."

"You don't say." Sabrina had to admit, the thought of Aaron close by made her feel a lot safer. "I'd better go."

"We'll drive with you," Jessie said, in a tone that indicated she wasn't going to take no for an answer. The trail was within walking distance, but they all knew that the sooner she got there, the better. Aaron, given his disappearing act into the woods a few minutes earlier, would undoubtedly get there on foot.

The three of them got into Sabrina's Jeep, Jessie sitting in the back, and drove in silence to the trailhead. It would take Sabrina about fifteen minutes to get to the place that had been Rosie Donovan's point last seen—the tip of the figure-eight loop the trail made that was just past the Dungeness Falls. Rosie had gone on the easy hike alone six months ago, though she'd run into some friends near the little wooden fence that surrounded the best observation point on the path from which to view the falls. She'd stopped to talk to them for a bit and had continued on her way, and that had been the last time anyone had seen her.

Sabrina pulled her Jeep into one of the four parking spots at the trailhead, which was marked by a small brown park sign with a hiker silhouette on it. She got out, grabbing her pack and walking stick.

As soon as she'd closed the Jeep door, Jessie jumped out of the back and threw her arms around Sabrina. "Be careful, okay? This whole thing really freaks me out."

Sabrina patted her gently on the back, surprised at the sudden show of emotion, even from the perpetually sensitive Jessie. "You know, *you're* starting to freak me out with this doomsday act of yours."

"You'll be fine." Alex lightly smacked her arm with the back of his hand after Jessie let her go, the closest he came to genuine affection. "You're the best in the state. And your friend, the walking carpet, will be there to snipe anyone who gives you trouble."

"Right." She turned to look at the start of the trail. It was always a little surprising how much light the forest canopy blocked out once you left the road and were under it. She couldn't help but dread that moment when she'd step onto the trail and the forest would pretty much swallow her up—and she'd be all alone.

As if sensing her fear, Alex put his hands on her shoulders and squeezed. Jessie patted her back.

"Excuse me." A tall man in khaki cargo shorts and a long-sleeved shirt made of moisture-wicking nylon brushed past her as he stepped off the road and onto the trail. His face was partially obscured by a Mariners baseball cap, the brim of which he touched as he walked past, giving them a slight smile of greeting. One of the undercover cops who were supposed to be in the area posing as hikers? Had to be. The cops were under orders to keep to the grass on the sides of the trails and not to go too far ahead of her, so if he was undercover and assigned to this area she'd see him again.

She said goodbye to Alex and Jessie, and

for the first time in months—maybe even in over a year—she hit the trail without either of them beside her. She clung so hard to her walking stick, her nails dug into her thumb. It was a little hard and thin to be a security blanket, but that's how she felt about it at that moment.

It was a rare sunny fall day, and the light filtered through the trees to dapple the pathway before her. There was no sign of the hiker who'd passed her earlier, but then, Dungeness was a pretty winding stretch. For all she knew, he could be around the corner.

She heard a rustling noise to her right, and then a fat, gray possum waddled out of a hollow log to twitch its nose at her before waddling away again. Birds were fluttering in the canopy overhead, the calls of several different species creating a cacophony of birdsong. It would have been a lovely hike, if her overall purpose weren't so grim. She looked around to see if she could spot Aaron, but she couldn't see even a hint of him or his weird, fuzzy suit. For all she knew, she'd walked over him at some point and hadn't even noticed.

Keeping her pace brisk, she reached the

top of the trail where it connected with the Dungeness River in less than ten minutes. Just before she reached the lookout, the water came into view, gurgling pleasantly over a series of river rocks covered in moist green moss. The part of the river visible from the trail was fairly narrow and shallow, with the exception of the pool at the bottom of the falls, which was deep enough to swim in if you liked ice-cold water.

She slowed her pace, scanning the mess of footprints on the ground for any sign that someone had been here and had left her a message. Finally reaching the lookout to the falls, she stretched her hand out and skimmed it along the scratchy wooden fence as she stared at the dusty ground.

There.

Right next to the far end of the fence from where she was standing was a perfect footprint, the tread stamped so far into the dirt, she knew someone had planted the print deliberately. Her heart hammering in her ears, the river drowning out all sound around her, she got out her tape measure and made a beeline for it.

A perfect match, from the zigzag pattern

on the sole to the length and width measurements to the wear patterns on the heel. This was their guy, all right. She'd read his message correctly.

Now if she could just shake the feeling that he was watching her. From her perch on the ground, she checked out the area. The path behind her was deserted, up until the point where it curved about a hundred yards back and disappeared into the trees. Nothing human appeared to break up the green and brown landscape of the forest to her left. To her right was the river, which wasn't crossable at this point without going for a very cold swim, so she assumed he hadn't done that. The rocks on the sides of the falls were slick with water and highly dangerous to anyone who chose to climb them, so she didn't worry about him being there, either.

But he could have taken a circuitous route to the top of the falls. He could be somewhere up ahead, waiting for her.

Whose woods these are, I think I know.

"Stop it. You were the one who insisted on doing this." Rubbing both hands up and down her cheeks, she mentally checked herself. Cowering here wasn't going to get them any closer to finding this guy. Using her walking stick for leverage, she pushed herself up to stand and looked for the next print.

It wasn't there.

Come on. It has to be here. He didn't float in to leave this one track. She scanned the immediate area around the boot print, but a second track wasn't jumping out at her, even though it should have been, given the fine layer of dirt over this portion of the path.

Okay, do what you do best. Cut for sign.

She started working in a zigzag pattern, taking what she figured was the Overman's most likely route. After about fifteen minutes, she finally spotted a prominent heel curve on the edge of the trail, several feet north of the falls lookout. A hint of the zigzag tread showed up in the dirt. Judging by the placement, horizontal to the trail and half in the grass, it looked like he might be headed off the beaten path. She cut for sign again, found a cluster of mashed plants.

And another cluster just beyond those that looked like they'd been mashed and then fluffed back up again by hand to hide the fact that someone had been there.

"He's obscuring his trail," she murmured. Of course he wasn't going to make this easy. She headed back to the last print in the dirt, and sure enough, now that she was looking for it, she noticed that the dirt around the heel curve impression had been swept, probably with a leafy branch, to get rid of his other tracks.

Cursing a blue streak in Spanish, Sabrina went back into the tall grass, to continue.

Several hours passed, during which she painstakingly tracked the Overman, print by nearly-invisible print. At one point, the trail led her in a false direction, and it wasn't until she'd been following it for half an hour that she noticed he'd backed up inside the prints he'd left going forward, intending to leave her at a dead end. So she'd back-tracked along the double trail until she found another track hidden in the brush, heading off in another direction entirely. He led her in circles, across the river and back, and over to Black Wolf Run, where she found the only other complete print of the entire journey, next to Hot Spring Seven. Then, she wound down to the logging road, through the thick, briar-filled woods to

Thunderhead Way, and down a fairly easy stretch to the point where it intersected with Mosley Gap Trail.

By the time she hit the place where Jennifer Jenkins's campsite had been, her body ached from exhaustion, and her eyes were scratchy with fatigue. Reaching up, she rubbed the back of her neck and considered sitting down for a moment. On the one hand, she needed the rest. On the other, what if he were watching her? What if he took her stopping as the sign of weakness he'd been looking for, and came on the attack? The way she saw it, she had only one option—keep moving.

She followed the miniscule sign past Jennifer's campsite and down through the trees in the same direction she'd traveled before when he'd chased her. The woods around her were eerily silent, which couldn't be a good sign. Maybe the animals knew something—or saw something—she didn't. Maybe she was getting close.

Every tree seemed like a potential hiding place. Every bend in the trail terrified her. Every step she took, she expected him to jump out at her, to materialize from the green-and-brown monotony of her surroundings. She'd been hiking for nearly the entire day, and the light was just starting to fade in the late afternoon. How long until she could no longer see? How long until she found what he'd wanted her to find?

How long until he stepped out into the open and came for her?

She expected the trail to head toward the incline she'd tumbled down last time she was up here, but instead it veered unexpectedly in the opposite direction. The tracks were becoming clearer, her eye fatigue aside.

Maybe you're close. Maybe you'll find what he wants you to find.

She pushed on, through a stand of birch trees and a thick clump of tall grasses, behind which sat a small pond. The tracks were more than obvious here—they were practically leaping out at her. He'd pretty much stomped in a circle, all the way around the tiny pool of water.

I'm here. Now what?

Gripping her walking stick with both hands, she planted it in the soft dirt, leaning her weight against it. He'd walked in a circle. What was here?

Oh, God, what if she was supposed to find something at the bottom of the water?

She pushed the thought out of her mind, leaning against the tall, thin trunk of an evergreen. She was so tired, her body just couldn't go anymore. Not without rest. Maybe if she just stood here for a moment, just closed her eyes for a second…

Suddenly, every sense went on high alert, and her eyes popped open. She didn't know what set her off, but that didn't matter now. She scanned her surroundings, and her fear magnified everything, every sound, every movement, until she couldn't even trust her eyes and ears.

The slightest flicker of movement in the trees over there.

A shadow passing through her peripheral vision.

A twig snapping behind her.

The dark shape by a fallen log.

But then she heard it, the faintest brush behind her, the sound that fabric made when it touched something, and she knew.

He's here.

"Sssabrina," a hoarse male voice whispered behind her.

Chapter Twelve

She screamed, whirling around to see who had murmured her name.

Oh, God, it was the man who had brushed against her at the trailhead. He had on the same clothing—cargo shorts and a long-sleeved shirt—but in place of the baseball cap he now wore his all-too-familiar ski mask. How had he eluded her this long? Her eyes traveled to his feet, and she knew he'd probably changed shoes, using the zigzag-treaded ones only to leave her the sign that she'd followed to this place.

Backing up almost involuntarily, she stumbled when her heels hit the soft, algae-coated mud at the edge of the pond.

"Come here, little bird, just a little further," he crooned, moving toward her.

"No," she whispered, edging sideways around the pond.

"Over here. You've done so well."

Her gaze dropped to his hands, the hands that had broken Jennifer Jenkins's neck, and she started at the sight of the syringe he held. He was going to drug her, and then she'd be his, for however long he chose to keep her alive.

"No!" she shouted.

A loud rustling sounded from off to her right, and when she glanced that way, she saw the moss hanging off a hemlock tree suddenly come to life, suddenly lift what might have been a gun in her direction.

Aaron.

The Overman started laughing.

"Sabrina, run!" Aaron shouted. And because she knew she was blocking his line of fire, she did. She tore through the mud around the side of the pond and then darted into the woods, twigs snapping and leaves crackling under her feet. A patch of brighter-than-usual light shone through the trees on the far side of the pond, and she headed for it.

Behind her, she heard the crack of Aaron's gun as he fired it, and she automatically turned her head toward the sound. Just then, her shins came into contact with something soft, but substantial, and she lost her balance. As she fell, she pitched her arms forward to catch herself and closed her eyes.

Her knees hit the dirt first, the pain radiating through her legs, and then her hands slammed into the ground. Her arms buckled, and she fell hard onto her chest, the impact knocking the breath out of her.

She rolled onto her side, eyes watering as she struggled to take in air again, and that's when she noticed that the thing she'd stumbled over wasn't a thing at all, but a person.

Finally managing to inhale, Sabrina pushed off the ground and sat up, every muscle in her body shaking from the effort. She dragged herself over to the prone figure, coughing as she moved.

It was a woman, and she was completely still. Her back was to Sabrina, and she was mostly covered by a filthy green blanket. A pair of delicate-looking feet stuck out from the bottom, and at the top she could see a few stray locks of long black hair. Sabrina reached out and peeled the blanket back, her hands automatically gripping the woman's wrist to feel for a pulse. Her skin was so cold.

When she couldn't find one right away, she tugged on the woman's shoulder, until the woman fell over on her back, her dark hair obscuring her face. Sabrina reached up to touch her neck, hoping that she'd find the carotid pulse, strong and true under the skin there. Her movement knocked some of the woman's hair out of her face.

Not a woman at all, but a young girl.

And her skin was like ice.

"Rosie," she whispered, covering her mouth with her hand. "Oh, Aaron. Oh, no."

FOR THE first time in his life, Aaron missed a target. Not that part of him hadn't wanted to end the sorry bastard's life then and there, but he knew that killing him would mean the Overman would take the story of what had happened to his daughter with him to his grave. And Aaron couldn't risk never knowing, especially if the man had Rosie hidden somewhere, still alive. He couldn't risk leaving her possibly to die slowly, locked up in a secret location where no one could find her.

So when he took the shot, he aimed for

the Overman's knee, not the head or the heart. But the warning he'd given Sabrina to get out of the line of fire had given the man enough time to get out of the way. Judging by the fact that he was now running away, Aaron had only grazed him, if that.

Aaron lifted his rifle to take another shot, but there were too many trees between them. Not wanting to risk losing his only lead to his daughter's whereabouts, Aaron took off running in pursuit.

His feet sticking in the soft ground, he dodged saplings and ducked under branches, keeping his focus solely on the figure several yards in front of him. He pushed himself faster than he'd ever run in his life, knowing that the man before him held the key to finding his daughter. His legs burned, and he told himself to take the pain and keep going.

The killer curved to the right, disappearing from view behind a clump of bushes. Aaron pushed himself harder and ate up the distance, making the same turn himself. He thought that once he cleared the bushes, the man would be visible again.

He wasn't.

Aaron kept going, but soon he realized that he was in pursuit of nothing. Skidding to a halt, he turned in a circle, scanning his surroundings. Once, twice, three times, and still nothing. Not a movement, not a sound.

Frustration gave way to sheer panic as he realized just how much he'd lost in that chase. He backtracked, staring at the ground and frantically hoping he'd see something that would tell him what just happened, some sign that would get him back on the man's tail again.

He wasn't a tracker, and he couldn't read a thing from the ground.

Swearing viciously, he punched the nearest tree trunk, the rough bark digging into the skin on his knuckles. Sharp tears sprang to his eyes, and he gasped for air, something hard, and large, and painful settling in his chest and refusing to give way.

He couldn't have lost her. Not now, not when he was so close.

"Aaron!"

The sound of Sabrina's voice brought him back. Whatever he'd done, whatever he'd lost, she was here now, and she sounded like she was in trouble. Getting himself under control as much as he could, he headed in her direction.

"Aaron!"

He could see a clearing up ahead, hear the sound of someone coming toward him, not bothering to disguise their movements. And then Sabrina stepped into an opening between the trees, the last of the day's sunlight streaming behind her.

He moved to go to her, and then someone else stepped into the light. He froze, unable to believe, to really believe what his eyes were telling him, what his heart already knew.

"Rosie," he breathed.

She didn't look seriously hurt, not on the outside, but he knew his baby girl wasn't anywhere close to the same person she'd been six months ago. He'd never seen her like this, subdued, quiet, her eyes darting around like a frightened animal as she clutched a disgusting, scratchy blanket around her too-thin frame. The mischievous sparkle he'd always loved about her was completely, utterly gone.

He stepped forward, slowly, carefully, because he didn't want to scare her, didn't know how to deal with this new person he saw in his daughter's eyes. His heart was so full, he could barely breathe.

Then he noticed that she was clinging to Sabrina, her fingers in a white-knuckled death grip around Sabrina's elbow. No. No, no, no, that monster couldn't have made his daughter this afraid, made his brave girl curl up into herself, so that her own father would terrify her. He pressed his lips together, wondering what he could say, what he could do to show her she was safe. "Baby girl," he choked out. *Please be okay. You have to be okay.*

He moved closer, reached for her, his too-empty arms aching to hold his little girl after so long. But she planted one hand against his chest in a feeble attempt to push him away.

Not wanting to upset her, he reluctantly stepped back. And instead of saying something, doing anything, she slowly moved her hand in front of her face, splaying her fingers and looking at them almost as if she were confused by them. It was an odd gesture, and it made him wonder whether she was drugged, or whether she'd just— oh, God—had he driven her mad?

"Daddy," she said simply, slowly, still staring at her hand.

"What—" He swallowed, trying to get his voice under control. "What is it, baby?"

She inched her hand toward him, the forward movement so slow, it was almost imperceptible. He could see blood on her nails, and the old, helpless anger flashed through him once more.

"Daddy," she said again. She lifted her arm so her hand was near his face.

He reached out and held her palm in both of his hands, stroking it comfortingly with his thumb. And then he saw it.

There was blood under the nails of her first two fingers. Blood, and a small shred of what might be skin. Someone else's skin.

Her head lifted, and just for a second, some of her old fire showed in her expression, in the angle of her dirt-streaked chin. And then somehow, by some miracle, she was in his arms, and he was holding her, stroking her tangled hair, and he didn't worry at that moment about fixing anything—he just clung to his daughter for the first time in too long, offering her the same refuge he always had, where fathers were strong and brave and could make the worst nightmares go away.

"Baby, you're the strongest—" he paused when his voice broke "—smartest girl I know. One scratch, and you just gave us everything."

SABRINA RADIOED for police and medical assistance to escort Rosie down the mountain, briefly explaining their confrontation with the Overman to Skylar. She also relayed a message from Aaron, telling Skylar to get the police to set up roadblocks at every gate in the hopes that they could catch the creep on his way out.

The EMTs were the first on the scene, and after checking on Rosie's immediate condition, they strapped her to a stretcher, telling Aaron and Sabrina that she'd been heavily drugged. Aaron borrowed an evidence collection kit from one of the first police officers to arrive at the scene and took a fingernail scraping from Rosie, taking care to preserve the DNA evidence she'd obviously fought hard to obtain.

The ambulance was waiting at the trailhead when they got down the mountain, ready to take off as soon as Rosie was inside. Without saying a word to Sabrina, Aaron got inside with his daughter, and the EMTs shut the door behind them, scurrying to the front of the vehicle and scrambling inside. The driver turned the lights and siren on and quickly pulled out of the parking area, heading for Port Renegade General Hospital.

Which was exactly as it should be. She didn't blame Aaron for focusing everything he had on his daughter. In fact, all she herself could think about was Rosie—how different she looked from the vivacious girl Aaron had described, how sickly and timid she seemed.

What did that man do to you?

She had no idea, but the things she was imagining terrified her. She watched the flashing lights of the ambulance fade into the darkness, and she wondered. How do you recover from something like that? How do you spend six months with someone who wants to hurt you, someone who's willing to kill, and ever go back to being the person you were before? How do you deal with extended trauma like that and go on afterwards without being afraid of everything and everyone? She couldn't imagine.

How do you survive six months with a madman when no one is looking for you but your father?

She steepled her hands in front of her mouth, trying to stifle the urge to cry. "I'm so sorry," she whispered into her fingers.

"I don't know what you're sorry for, but you're my freakin' hero," a voice said behind her. She turned around and came face-to-face with Eddie Ventaglia, who smiled at her sheepishly.

"Look, I know I didn't do wonders for the relationship between SAR and the Port Renegade PD after Rosie disappeared, but I hope you'll accept my apology." He adjusted his tie, dropped his hands, and then moved them up to toy with it again.

She blinked back the moisture in her eyes, trying to absorb what Ventaglia was telling her. "Of course, Detective. I understand."

"Call me Eddie," he said. "You know, Aaron radioed your position in all day so our officers could keep track of you. Now that I've pretty much gotten a blow-by-blow of how hard you work, I will never doubt that you haven't put your all into a search, ever again. Even if it's my wife that goes missing, God forbid."

"Yeah, well, Aaron was right. Rosie was alive all this time, and she was waiting for someone to find her." Sabrina tried to push the thoughts of what Rosie had been through out of her head, but the images her imagination conjured up wouldn't leave her alone.

"Don't beat yourself up. He's a smart one, our guy." Eddie laid a hand on her shoulder. "Had a small off-road bike waiting on one of the old logging roads, and he drove it through the park to the highway. Left it by the fence and either hitched a ride or walked into town. We've got patrol cars searching up and down for him, but I think we lost him."

She closed her eyes briefly. "Oh, no."

Eddie's shoulders sagged a little. "I know. We'll catch him, but I just hope it's before he goes after someone else, you know? Hey, you look like you need to sit down. Do you think if I drove you somewhere with good coffee and some killer donuts you'd be able to tell me the details about what happened?"

"Sure. Actually, could we just sit in your car. Like, now?" She didn't know how much longer she could stay on her feet, every muscle in her body was cramping now that she'd held still for more than a minute.

Eddie offered her his arm and helped her to his nearby Crown Victoria. He opened the passenger-side door and deposited her inside, so she sat on the seat with her feet on the ground outside. Leaning against another Crown Vic parked beside his, he got out a notebook. "So, what happened after you started off down the first trail?"

Someone produced a thermos mug full of lukewarm coffee, which Sabrina gratefully accepted. Wrapping her hands around the small plastic cup, she gave Eddie all of the details, ending with one very important one.

"Here's the thing I haven't had the chance to tell Aaron yet. I'm pretty sure the Overman had an accomplice."

Eddie looked up from his notebook. "Seriously? What makes you so sure?"

"I didn't realize it at first, but after a while I noticed that there were other prints everywhere his were. Not the obvious tracks that he made with the boots he wore when he took Rosie and Tara, but the tracks he was trying to hide. There were always print smudges next to them with a different pattern." She took a sip of the coffee, trying not to grimace at the cool temperature because she desperately needed the caffeine. "It makes sense—that's how he moved so quickly, always staying ahead of me to lay the trail while someone else obscured it and made it hard for me."

Eddie scratched his chin. "Hmmm. Maybe it's time for Aaron and me to pay Mr. Witkowski another visit."

"I think that's a good idea. Someone's helping this guy, which means that someone else knows where Tara is."

Chapter Thirteen

Dean Witkowski didn't even see them coming.

When Aaron and Eddie knocked on his door, the guy answered it, pleasant as could be, as if he had nothing to hide.

"Well, hey, Dean. We'd like to talk to you for a minute," Eddie said. "May we come in?" Without waiting for an answer, Eddie shoved past him and went inside his little hovel of an apartment.

They'd held him for having Rosie's jacket as long as they could, but without any more evidence to tie him to Rosie's disappearance, they couldn't arrest him and ultimately had to let him go. Sabrina's accomplice theory, however, gave them a whole new line of questioning to pursue. And finding him at his apartment, as long as he didn't ask them to leave, was even better. They might get lucky and find a pile of evidence just sitting on his coffee table.

"What's this all about?" Dean whined as he shut the door behind them. "I told you how I got that jacket."

"Oh, we know. This is something else entirely, Dean," Eddie said.

"Where were you yesterday?" Aaron asked, firing the question at the little man like a bullet.

"When?" He squinted at them, already puzzled by the line of questioning.

"Pretty much all day, Witkowski," Aaron snapped. It was satisfying to play bad cop in front of this little twit. It'd be even more satisfying to intimidate him into incriminating himself.

"I was at work. I woke up, ate breakfast, took the six-twenty bus, and was at the day care where I work as a custodian by seven." He sat down on the sagging cushions of a pea-green couch that had seen better days. "My boss can tell you, I was there all day."

He gestured to the two detectives to sit, and then he looked at Aaron, tilting his head as he seemed to be attempting to see right through him. "You found her, didn't you? Your daughter?"

"And how would you know that?" Eddie asked, planting his bulk next to Dean on the couch.

Witkowski waved his hand around for a minute, trying to find the right words. "I sensed it. You look like you're at peace, none of that disturbing, frantic energy coming off of you in waves. I don't feel like you're sucking the life out of me anymore."

"Oh, I'm ready to do plenty of life-sucking, Witkowski, trust me on that," Aaron said, still positive that he knew Rosie had been found because he'd been there, not because of any psychic powers he had.

"Look, call my boss. She can tell you I was there. Can we end this now?"

His eyes shifted to a door at the far end of the apartment, and Aaron realized it wasn't the first time the man had looked in that direction. He might not have believed in psychic abilities, but he believed in cop sense, and his was going off the charts right now. He moved to the other side of the room. "Do you mind if I use your bathroom?" Putting his hand on the knob, he turned it and pushed through before Witkowski could do more than yelp.

Inside was a small office. And on the wall just above the little scratch-and-dent wooden desk were hundreds of newspaper clippings, some originals, some copies and several that were duplicated—all focusing on Tara Fisher and Rosie.

"Eddie," he said calmly, "I think we might have found our accomplice. Someone has himself a trophy room."

"I'M LOOKING for Rosie Donovan, please."

The nurse looked up from the chart she'd been reading and smiled pleasantly. "Third door down on your left. Poor little thing. She hasn't said a word since we brought her in here." She clicked her tongue, shaking her head.

Thanking her, Sabrina walked down the hall, the smell of antiseptic and alcohol irritating her nostrils. When she reached the third door on the left, she paused with her hand on the metal doorjamb, peering inside.

Rosie lay on her bed, the head of which was raised up. The small, flat-screen television that was attached to a swinging arm beside her bed was in front of her for optimal viewing, but she was instead looking out the window, a sad, thoughtful expression on her young face. She appeared to be alone.

Taking a deep breath, Sabrina entered the room.

Rosie blinked in surprise when she saw her, then pushed the TV away, straightening her spine. Just as the nurse had said, she didn't say a word.

"I'm sorry I didn't call." Without drawing too much attention to them, Sabrina placed the small glass vase filled with pink roses on the table next to the window, then turned. "I just was passing by, and I thought I'd see how you were doing."

Rosie lifted a shoulder in a half-hearted shrug.

"Yeah, I'm sure everyone wants you to say fine, but you're not fine. I certainly wouldn't be fine." She walked over to the chair next to Rosie's bed. "Do you mind if I sit for a minute?"

The girl smiled without showing any teeth, and flipped a hand at the chair as if to say go ahead.

Perching on the edge of the vinyl-upholstered chair, Sabrina cupped her hands around her knees. She knew she had something to say, but it was hard to figure out how to say it. She took a deep breath, and just started spilling her guts, figuring she'd make sense at some point. "Rosie, you might not know who I am, but I work for Port Renegade Search and Rescue. I'm a tracker. I look at people's footprints and I can usually tell where they're going, and what they did when they got there." She smiled a little. "Within reason."

Tilting her head slightly, Rosie leaned back against the raised mattress, listening intently.

"I just—" Sabrina stopped, unable to continue for a moment. "I wanted to tell you how glad I am that you're safe. See, I've been looking for you for a long time. But…"

Now here was the hard part. "But when you disappeared, I was in charge of one of the tracking teams, and after a couple of weeks when we couldn't find you— Oh, God." She swiped at her eyes, which were filling up with tears. "I persuaded my supervisor to call off the search. We had a couple of hikers from Tacoma who got lost, and I just didn't think we had enough people to keep going when we didn't have any leads."

She sniffled, then grabbed a tissue out of a nearby box, twisting it in her hands instead of using it. "I'm glad you're back safe, and I wanted you to know I'm so, so sorry I didn't do my job better. That you were alone, with that madman, for so long, and I cut off everyone who was looking for you, except your father—"

Sabrina was crying in earnest now, tears streaming down her cheeks, and she couldn't look at the young girl before her. "Your father's an amazing man, you know? He never stopped looking for you. He knew you were still alive, and he never gave up." The tissue had turned into a soggy little lump in her hand, and she set it on the register behind her. "I'm not asking you to forgive me. I just thought you deserved an apology. You deserved more than that." Grabbing the purse she'd carried in with her, Sabrina slung it over her shoulder, clinging to the strap and feeling small and stupid in front of this young woman who'd been through way too much. "Thank you for seeing me."

With that, she stumbled out of the room, walking down the hallway as fast as she could without making a scene.

STANDING by the doorway to Rosie's room, his hands filled with his daughter's favorite kinds of candy from the machine on the first floor, Aaron felt as if someone had punched him in the gut after he heard what Sabrina had to say. When she left, bursting out of the room so quickly she didn't even see him, he simply tossed the candy into Rosie's room and followed her. He caught her gently by the arms just after she'd pushed through the door to the stairwell.

"What was that, Sabrina?"

"Leave me alone, Aaron," she said, without malice. "That wasn't meant for you to hear."

"What, that you blame yourself for what that man did to her? That you're beating yourself up for making the best decision you could based on what you knew?" He cupped her cheek with his hand, and her face crumpled when he touched her.

"She reached out for you when you left." He paused letting his words sink in. "She doesn't blame you any more than I do."

Turning her head out of his grasp, Sabrina stared at the floor. "She should. You did."

"I was an idiot. I'm so sorry I laid all that on your shoulders." He put his arms around her, pulling her to him. She was stiff at first, but after a few seconds, she relaxed against him, and he just held her. It felt right. It felt like coming home.

"You were amazing yesterday. You just wouldn't quit. When other people would've fallen down from exhaustion or passed out from fear, you kept going. You think I didn't see that you'd walk through fire for someone if you had to?"

She tucked her hands around her face and cried. He just held her tighter.

"I know you, Sabrina. Other than my daughter, you're the best person I know."

She shook her head, her face still buried in his chest. "No. I'm not, Aaron."

"You are," he said softly. "And I love you."

She raised her head then, staring at him with a combination of guilt and wonder, and he thought she'd never looked more beautiful. "For everything you did, and everything you are. Even if—" He stopped, unable to put the worst of his fears into words. "Even if the worst had happened, I would still thank you every day for what you've done. None of what happened to Rosie, or Tara or Jennifer is your fault."

He bent down, kissed her softly, and she sighed into his lips, closed her eyes. "Believe it," he whispered.

Her eyes fluttered open, and she regarded him quietly for a moment. "Thank you," she said simply.

He smiled, reluctant to let her go, but knowing that he had to get back to his daughter. He took his hands off her waist, letting them fall at his sides. "It's always been just the two of us, since Rosie's mother left us." He shoved his hands in his pockets, inwardly pleading with her to understand. "I think I knew from the start that she would go—she had some psychological problems that just got worse after Rosie was born. So the minute the nurses put this fat little baby with this big thatch of hair on her head in my arms, I thought, 'Here we go, baby girl. I don't know how, but here we go.'"

She nodded. "It's not our time now. I know that, Aaron. Your daughter needs you, and she will for a long time, after what she's been through." She lifted a hand, laid it on the side of his face. He closed his eyes and leaned into her touch. "I'm here. Whenever you need me. No matter how long it takes." He turned his head, pressed his lips to the palm of her hand.

"You should know," he said carefully, "this guy was looking for you. Rosie said he didn't intend to leave her behind—I spoiled his plans when I showed up and shot at him. He planned to exhaust you and then use her to lure you back to wherever he held her, and is still holding Tara. He wants you."

He looked like he wanted to split himself in half, and Sabrina knew that while he needed to go to his daughter, he wanted to protect her, too. "I'll be fine," she assured him.

"I'm sending a couple of officers with you. They're under orders not to let you out of their sights."

She opened the door, then put her hand on his shoulder, guiding him back toward the hospital room where Rosie was resting.

"Go," she whispered. "She really needs you."

He nodded. And left.

Chapter Fourteen

The police were still holding Witkowski the next day, but Aaron knew they didn't have enough to keep him, and the thought frustrated the hell out of him. He had a rock-solid alibi, and all signs were pointing to his simply being a weirdo obsessed with Rosie's and Tara's disappearances.

What they did have was a DNA profile of the Overman, thanks to Rosie's strength of character. They'd managed to get a rush on it at the lab, and Eddie had just called him at the hospital to let him know that they'd gotten a hit on CODIS, the FBI's DNA database. It belonged to one James McAdams, a Gulf War veteran and former Army Ranger who'd gotten a dishonorable discharge for getting into a knock-down, drag-out fight with one of his supervisors.

He'd been in and out of work as a welder, his temper and superior attitude managing to get him fired from just about every job he'd ever had. And he'd been suspected of beating a young college co-ed beyond recognition a few years back after following her to her apartment from a bar in Seattle. The only things they had on him were the victim's description and DNA evidence, and when the lab had screwed up the crime-scene sample, they didn't have that. So McAdams had walked, but his DNA profile remained in CODIS, waiting for this moment.

They had him. They had a name, an address, and the make, model, and license plate of his one and only car—which was sold with tires matching the track they'd cast at the end of Tara Fisher's trail. Now they just had to catch him.

Aaron left it up to Eddie and the rest of his colleagues to find McAdams and the identity of his accomplice, preferring instead to stay with Rosie until the man was caught. As elated as he was to have her back, he hated, hated what that man had done to her, would have given anything to have taken her place, to have his innocent girl back again, instead of this quiet, all-too-knowing woman.

The sound of someone clearing her throat made him look up from the book he'd been reading while Rosie slept. Sabrina stood in the doorway and, much as he wanted to save this time for Rosie, he was glad to see her.

"I can't stay. I just brought Rosie some books." She set a plastic bag filled with paperbacks on the chair nearest the door. "I remember how you said she loves to read, and I thought maybe she could use something until they let her out of here."

"Thanks," he said, getting up and walking toward her. "I'll tell her they're from you."

"How is she?"

"She's talking to me. She told me a little about what she's been through, but there's a lot she won't say." But the things she did say felt like ice picks straight to his heart. "She wasn't raped, at least—apparently he had some sort of anatomical issue."

Sabrina bit her lip, her brow furrowed at the disturbing visuals he was no doubt planting in her head. He knew, because he saw those same visuals constantly. "But he liked to hurt them. He got off on having power over them." He told her about the DNA results and what they'd found out about James McAdams, then turned and looked at his daughter, sleeping peacefully, connected to an IV and several monitors. She'd been severely dehydrated when they'd found her, not to mention pumped full of a cocktail of powerful painkillers that had made it difficult for her to function until they wore off.

"I'm glad you're close to catching him—" She broke off, looking at the figure on the hospital bed. "I'm so sorry. No one should have to go through what you and she went through."

The sound of footsteps slapping down the hallway had them both heading for the door to see what was coming their way. Sabrina nearly collided with Alex, who ran inside, clearly out of breath. Eddie Ventaglia hurried in close behind him.

"Bree, I've been trying to get you on your cell," he panted. "Jessie's missing."

Sabrina gasped as Aaron looked to Eddie for confirmation. "We've had reports of our guy traveling down 101 in a white Ford, registered in his name, with an unidentified woman. They anticipated one of our roadblocks and exited the vehicle and are continuing on foot up into the mountains." He turned to Sabrina. "That's why I'm here. We need your expertise. Skylar's in my car downstairs. She'll be your third, and Aaron, we can leave an officer here if you want to go in as backup for them."

Aaron looked at his daughter, sleeping peacefully. He didn't want to leave her, but he wanted her to wake up knowing that James McAdams was safely locked up somewhere where he wouldn't hurt her or another young woman again. "I'll go," he said.

"But Jessie, what? What's going on?" Sabrina was shaking her head, apparently unable to process what they were telling her. "McAdams has her?"

"Yeah, she— Wait. Did you say McAdams?" Alex asked.

"We got an ID this morning from DNA," Aaron supplied.

"Oh, crap." Alex pulled his hand down the side of his face, his expression growing more worried by the minute. "McAdams is the name of her ex-husband." The four of them were silent for a minute as they processed that new information. For his part, Aaron couldn't believe they'd missed something like that. "You don't think—?"

"We haven't gotten that far into his background yet, but it could be. We do know that he's divorced," Eddie said.

"So her ex-husband could be the one who has her? She never talked about him," Sabrina said. "Did she ever tell you he was dangerous, Alex?"

He shook his head.

"You should know that witnesses saw a white sedan parked in front of Jessie's house this morning, and there were no signs of foul play when we went inside," Eddie said.

"What does that mean? Her tracks weren't rushed and didn't show signs of panic, either," Alex added, his expressions grim. Sabrina looked at him, and he hated the possibility blooming in his head, the one he was going to have to share with her, so she could protect herself.

"Sabrina, it could mean that she went with him willingly," he told her gently. "Wilkowski might really be just a nut who inserted himself into the case. And Jessie

might be the accomplice you thought
McAdams has had all along."

SABRINA RODE in the back seat of Eddie's
car in silence, staring out the window and
wondering how things had come to this.
Could it really have been Jessie who had
obscured McAdams's prints while he'd led
her on that exhausting trek throughout the
park, just before attacking her? Had she disappeared on purpose the day they'd found
Jennifer, to allow McAdams a chance at
Sabrina?

But why? Why would she do such a
thing? Sabrina had not only liked Jessie,
she'd trusted her. Implicitly. She couldn't
believe her intuition could be so off about
someone. She would have left her nieces
alone with the woman, for heaven's
sake. The whole sorry situation made her
head throb.

It was nearly dark by the time they got
to the site. Skylar was already there
waiting for them, ready to take Jessie's
place. She had flashlights and walking
sticks with her, and she'd even brought
Sabrina a spare pair of hiking boots. The
area was crawling with state troopers and

Port Renegade Police, who'd set up large searchlights to illuminate the white Ford Focus at the side of the road.

"There's a K-9 unit that's been on the scene already," Aaron told her as he checked the sight on his rifle. "But the dogs are confused, for some reason. The handlers are telling me that they keep going in circles."

"He's throwing them off somehow," Sabrina said, looking around at the terrain, which was getting harder to see in the increasingly dim light. Pushing aside all thoughts of Jessie's possible betrayal—she'd believe it when she knew for sure—she stood and headed for the truck to get a look while Alex and Skylar readied the rest of their equipment.

The prints around the vehicle had been left mainly intact, other than a couple of dogs and their handlers tromping over a few portions. It was easy to see just what had happened here.

"McAdams and Jessie got out of the car here, as you know," she told Aaron and the other officers who were standing off to the side, watching her work in the glare of the spotlights. She pointed to the flurry of prints around the bumper. "They're each showing two different kinds of shoe patterns. It looks like they sat on the bumper here and changed into hiking boots. He may know exactly where he's going." She swallowed, feeling a chill as she looked at the story on the ground in front of her. "McAdams knows exactly what he's doing. His prints aren't hurried, like someone in a panic. He's walking at an even pace, and the woman he's with seems pretty calm, as well."

Alex moved in beside her, pointing to a rounded depression in the ground next to the truck's front bumper. "They probably have a bag of supplies with them. He may be planning to hole up in the woods some-where until we all go away."

"I'm not going anywhere," Skylar said as she joined them. Together, the three of them headed for a patch of weeds and brush that had a depression in the middle. The tracks said that that was where McAdams and Jessie had started walking.

"If he's not showing signs of panic, he's feeling confident," Aaron noted, getting into place behind them. "That makes him dangerous. Are you sure you want to do this?"

Sabrina looked at Skylar and Alex, who both nodded. "We're sure," she said. "Can you get the K-9 units off the field? We can separate their tracks from McAdams's, but it'd be easier if they stopped leaving more."

Aaron gave the order via radio, and she could hear the dogs barking as their handlers moved them off to the side. A full SWAT team fell in behind them as the four of them trudged into the weeds, Alex and Skylar's high-powered flashlights illuminating their way. Only Sabrina carried a walking stick, to use for rough measurements.

About a hundred yards into the brush, the tracks were no longer as obvious, and they came upon a small stream. She thought McAdams might have walked into the water to throw the dogs off, but a quick examination by flashlight told her that wasn't the case. He'd exited his car less than an hour ago—if they had gone through the stream, the silt they'd stirred up in the stream bed would still be clouding the surface. Instead, the water was crystal-clear.

Motioning to Alex to give her his flashlight, she shone the beam along the water, until she found an area that was cloudy. "They crossed here," she said, handing the light back. The four of them forded the shallow stream, and Sabrina picked up the trail again.

When they climbed a small rise, still outside of the cover of the trees up ahead, she noticed that they'd walked backward for a bit, obviously checking out the police that had been gathering around their abandoned vehicle. "They were here not too long ago," Skylar said, reading the sign without difficulty.

"They might still be close," Aaron warned. "Stay sharp."

Sabrina brought her hand up, rubbing her temple as she tried to ease the growing tension that had banded across her skull. McAdams had Jessie with him, and that fact alone gave him an advantage few fugitives had. It didn't take her long to realize that the dogs had become confused because she and McAdams had deliberately started walking on the dog tracks and on top of the officers' shoe prints. They'd walked in circles, hiding in some brush to let the dogs pass them, and then had continued in a different direction, criss-crossing the dogs' paths time and again.

Stopping under the cover of a tall willow near the stream bank, she waited for Aaron to catch up again and explained what she'd found to him. "They've spent most of their time going in circles," she whispered. "McAdams is close—I think he might even be able to see us."

She peered around in the near-darkness, the thick clouds overhead completely obscuring the moonlight. The only light they had to see by were their flashlights, and those also made them easy targets. If he had a gun with him, they could die before all of this was over. She could only hope that some decent part of Jessie's obviously insane mind would keep him from killing them all.

Her heart hammering inside her chest, her head throbbing in time with her pulse, she kept working through the night, Skylar and Alex by her side as they painstakingly moved from print to partial print, tumbled pebbles to flattened patch of grass, following each circle the pair made through the thick brush. Finally, the tracks led them into the trees at the base of a nearby hill, and they entered the forest. She hoped Aaron was looking up from time to time while the three of them had their eyes to the ground.

The radio Aaron carried flared to life, as Eddie started directing officers to ride on local school buses and escort them through roadblocks if they hadn't caught McAdams in the next couple of hours.

Unfortunately, they worked throughout the night with little to show for it. It was painstaking work, and her headache was this close to exploding into a full-blown migraine. The sky had just started to fade slightly when Sabrina noticed that dew had started to form on the grass at their feet. She crouched down to check out how it had affected the tracks, Alex moving in with his flashlight to assist.

Once she found what she was looking for, she motioned for them to be quiet and beckoned them closer. "Their feet knocked the dew off their tracks here," she whispered when they'd all formed a tight unit around the print. "He's been here within the last half hour. I'm guessing he's about a hundred feet from us right now, probably watching every move we're making." She turned to Aaron. "This is where we really need you."

He nodded, pulling his gun off his shoulders and holding it in both hands. "I'm moving up next to you." She didn't argue.

Sabrina squeezed her eyes open and shut, trying desperately to keep her vision from blurring. Reaching inside her pocket, she pulled out the bottle of ibuprofen and swallowed four pills dry for the second time that night.

"Bree, you want me to take point?" Skylar asked.

Pain ricocheted through her head as she nodded. "You'd better," she murmured, hating to give Skylar her too-vulnerable position but having no choice. However, when she turned to get into flank position, taking Skylar's flashlight, she saw something up ahead, obscured by the dark and the trees.

She'd seen too many of those in the last few days—bodies of young women lying on the ground. "Jessie."

She hadn't taken more than a couple of steps forward, intending to let the rest of the team catch up and get into place, when she noticed something strange in the ground. An arrow scratched hastily in the dirt, pointing to her right. She stopped, knowing that it was some sort of message, but her aching head made it hard to think, much less keep putting one foot in front of the other. She backed away, wondering how Jessie had made it without her ex-husband noticing.

Just then, McAdams stepped out of the brush and grabbed Sabrina around the neck, his elbow nearly crushing her windpipe. She felt the muzzle of a gun press against her throbbing temple.

"Back off. All three of you, or she dies, and you'll never find the ones you're looking for," McAdams snarled.

Operating on pure adrenaline, Sabrina turned her hand and pushed his arm upward, but he caught her again before she could escape, grabbing her chin so hard, she knew he could kill her with just one twist of his hand. She stilled, the pain in her head nearly blinding her. Her eyes found Aaron, who'd raised his rifle to his shoulder.

"Uh-uh, little bird," McAdams said. "I'd hate for this to end so soon."

"Let her go, McAdams. It's over," Aaron said calmly, squinting through his rifle's scope with his finger hovering over the trigger.

"Your pathetic rules don't apply to me," McAdams replied. "I'll shoot her in the head before you can even pull the trigger." He ducked behind her, using her for cover. Alex and Skylar stood by, horrified, illuminating the entire twisted scene with their lights. "And that would be a shame," he whispered in her ear. "You could transcend all of them."

Her head hurt and her entire body ached and her eyes were so tired, she could barely see. But Sabrina knew this had to end, and she knew she had to give Aaron permission to do it. The shot was risky, but they had to take the chance, had to hope that Jessie was alive and could tell them where Tara was.

"Aaron, can you make this?" She squinted, focusing with all of her energy so she could see what he did next.

He nodded, an almost imperceptible movement.

"Then do it."

Aaron pulled the trigger. Sabrina felt the bullet whoosh by her cheek, and she pulled away from the muzzle of McAdams's gun, catching him off guard so that he let her go. She dove to the ground just as McAdams's body jolted backward from the impact. He fell, the bullet having entered his head just behind his ear, shattering his skull.

Aaron ran up beside her. "God, Sabrina, are you all right?"

She squeezed the bridge of her nose, wanting to sink to the ground and sleep until the migraine left her. "Jessie," she murmured.

"She's okay." Alex came out from behind a tree, Jessie clinging to his arm. "He gave her a good thump on the head, but otherwise nothing's damaged."

"I'm so sorry, Sabrina," she sobbed, clinging to Alex. "I didn't know it was him until the day Tara disappeared. He came to my house and told me I had to help him, or he'd kill you and the girls he told me he was holding prisoner, and he'd never tell us where they were. He made me put something in Alex's water bottle to make him sick. He said he was going to kill all of you, and leave me alive to take the blame. I wanted to go to the police, but I was so scared." She turned to Aaron, pleading. "I thought if I could just find out where he was keeping the girls, then I could go to the police and protect you all. I'm sorry. I'm so sorry."

"Oh, Jess." Leaning on Aaron for support, Sabrina reached out and hugged the woman who'd been her friend for so long. "It's okay. You should have told us." James McAdams had played such a horrible game with so many women. Glancing at his lifeless body, lying in the shadows of the trees, she could only feel glad that he'd never terrorize anyone else again.

"But I know where he kept them now. He was going to take me there. Tara and another girl, a runaway. They're in an underground bunker that he built close to here." Jessie looked at Aaron, her expression almost triumphant. "Can you get that SWAT team up here, and I'll take you to them?"

Chapter Fifteen

A few months went by after they'd taken down McAdams. They'd found Tara and a runaway named Jill Simpson right where Jessie had said they'd be—in a horrific underground bunker McAdams had built inside the parklands just for the purpose of imprisoning his victims. Tara and Jill were in much the same condition as Rosie had been—dehydrated, frightened and no longer the same girls they'd been before McAdams had come into their lives. But both had been reunited with their families and were starting to rebuild their lives and their confidence.

McAdams had, like Hitler, perverted Nietzsche's Overman theories to justify his own sick penchant for hurting young girls. From interviews with the three victims and journals they'd discovered in the bunker, in his mind, he'd wanted to help them "evolve." What it really boiled down to, though, was that he was a simple sadist who got off on exerting total control over the girls he'd held captive. None of his victims, the police, or members of the SAR unit regretted that he was dead.

Jessie hadn't known about the Overman business—she'd just known that he'd seemed charming, handsome and perfect when they'd met, saying and doing all the right things until the day he'd hit her on their honeymoon. It had taken her a few months, but she'd gotten a divorce, changed her name and moved out of their Portland home, and had never looked back—until years later, when McAdams had found her in Port Renegade and had come back into her life in such a violent way. But instead of kidnapping her, McAdams used threats to control her, too, forcing her to help him. With McAdams gone, Jessie was opening up in a thousand different ways, the threat of her violent ex-husband gone from her life.

Sabrina hadn't seen much of Aaron. She missed him terribly, but she knew Rosie had a long road ahead of her, and Aaron had to dedicate as much time as he could to his daughter. So she just went back to life the way it had been before, finding lost hikers, joking with Alex, and trying to let Jessie know in a million ways that she didn't blame her for any of it. Jessie might not have done the right thing, but she'd done the best she could in an honest attempt to protect everyone. The authorities had seen it that way, too, as she'd been cleared of any wrongdoing in the McAdams case and was back working in SAR.

One freezing day in December, after no one had been lost in the park for weeks, the three of them had been asked to go up near Mosley Gap and measure tree trunks as part of one of the park rangers conservation programs.

"How are you feeling?" Jessie asked her as they walked out of the ranger station. "You looked like you were having a headache earlier."

One thing about Jessie, she had grown extra worried about everyone in her life, clucking over Alex and Sabrina like a proverbial mother hen.

"I'm fine, Jess," Sabrina replied patiently.

"Yes, you are fine," Alex piped up from behind them.

She spun around and started walking back to properly address him. "You do know, Alex, that if I ever decided to fire you for sexual harassment, that kind of talk won't get you far in corporate America?" She pulled her radio out of the pack and clipped it to her waistband. "Cubicles. Ties. And did I mention recycled air-conditioning?"

Alex gave a mock shudder at her words and then grinned at her. "I harass you out of the highest esteem for your intellect and tracking abilities, oh, fearless leader."

"Right." She faced forward once more, stopping in her tracks as she saw who was standing at the end of the parking lot.

"Rosie."

The teenager stood with her hands in the pockets of her oversized gray sweatshirt, smiling sheepishly as she scuffed the toe of her sneaker against the gravel. "Hi, Ms. Adelante. I was wondering if you had a second? I had a couple of quick questions."

She glanced at Alex and Jessie, who smiled at her and moved off to give them some privacy. "Of course. What can I do for you?" she said. She was tempted to go all Jessie on the girl and ask her how she was feeling, but she had a sense that Rosie wouldn't like the allusion to the horrors that she'd gone through. Better to concentrate on her as she was now.

"I've started thinking about what I want to do after I graduate, and I thought it might be cool to look into becoming a tracker." She shrugged, smiling. "I mean, my dad told me all about what you do, and I thought it sounded amazing. He said you would know if there were any internships or summer positions where I could maybe carry water for some tracking team and see what they do?"

Wow. Sabrina had to keep from responding for a minute, so she didn't start blubbering all over the poor girl. But she was nearly overcome with admiration. After all Rosie had been through, here she was, putting it behind her and moving on, as strong and brave as ever. "I've had apprentices before. Believe it or not, not that many people think creeping along the ground looking at footprints is all that exciting."

"A lot they know." Rosie smiled. Aaron was right—her huge, bright smile was like sunshine.

"I'd love to have you. I'll talk to Skylar, and you can probably start this summer, or on your next break from school if you want. Let me know when it is, and I'll schedule a state training then, so you can get some real hands-on advice from a lot of people."

"Cool!" Rosie bit her lower lip and winced apologetically. "After asking for that huge favor, I have one other thing to ask you."

"Sure."

The girl crossed her arms, staring at the ground and looking so much like her father, it took Sabrina's breath away. "You know, I still get nightmares. The horrible, screaming kind where Dad has to run in and talk me awake again."

"I don't doubt it, after what you've been through," Sabrina replied.

"And I'm scared, all the time. I hate being alone, and I can be a real pain in Dad's behind when he has to work nights."

Aaron had told her. In fact, she'd come to stay with Rosie one night when he'd had to go on duty and her grandmother hadn't been able to stay. Rosie hadn't even known that she'd been there—she'd slept the entire time, but Sabrina had been there in case the girl had had one of her nightmares. "Rosie, that's all understandable. I'd be a mess if I'd been through what you have."

Rosie took a deep breath, let it out, got up her nerve. "I've been seeing a counselor, to try to get through this, and we've talked about not letting McAdams continue to make me a victim." She looked Sabrina straight in the eye. "That means not letting my father be a victim of this anymore either." She widened her eyes as if she'd just said something huge.

"Okay," Sabrina agreed. "That makes sense."

Rosie laughed, rolling her eyes. "You don't get what I'm saying, do you?"

Smiling helplessly, Sabrina shook her head.

"My father misses you. I think he might be in love with you. And he's not dating you because of me. Which is stupid." Pulling a pair of sunglasses out of the front pocket of her sweatshirt, she put them on, turning her face to the sun, which was actually out, for once. "I'm asking you if you'd go out with my father. Please? At least just once, because I think he'd stop smothering me with his overprotective thing."

Sabrina laughed. "I have three brothers that you should meet, and then we can talk."

"Will you talk to him?"

"I'd love to talk to him," she replied.

"Good," a deep voice sounded behind her. Aaron stepped into her line of vision, and her pulse started to race at the mere sight of him.

"Going away now," Rosie said, and made a big show of creeping off toward the ranger station.

"Hey." Sabrina steepled her fingers in front of her mouth, smiling behind them like an idiot.

"Hey." He shoved his hands in his pockets, a smile playing on his own lips. They probably looked like two teenagers trying to ask each other to the prom. She didn't remember feeling this nervous around a guy since high school.

"So, there's something that's been bothering me."

She nodded, her heart too full to speak.

"Do you remember what I said to you when you asked me what would happen if I found Rosie?"

She inhaled deeply, looking at the trees, the ranger station building, Rosie walking along the other side of the parking lot—looking anywhere but directly at Aaron. "You said you'd show up on my doorstep and beg me to marry you." As much as she loved that idea, she knew the last thing Rosie needed was a new stepmother barging into their lives. "I'm not going to hold you to that, Aaron."

"I was hoping you would."

Her mouth dropped open, and she couldn't speak, even when he moved into her space and took her in his arms. He was still wearing his suit from work, so she reached up and straightened his tie, just to give her hands something to do. "How about a date first, Detective? I don't think we've ever had a real one."

"No, we haven't, have we?" He laughed softly, dropping his head to plant a kiss on her collarbone. "Where would you like to go?"

"Hmmm." She looked up at the sky in exaggerated thoughtfulness. "Somewhere hideously expensive. Where we have to dress up. Possibly with dancing."

He swallowed, smothering his knee-jerk grimace. "Okay, I can handle that."

"How about you and Rosie come over to my house tonight? I'll make a pizza, and we can catch her up on the TV she's missed." She shivered as his mouth traveled up to her neck.

"Love that idea. But Rosie's staying over at a friend's tonight." He raised his head, his expression a little more serious. "Part of her plan to not let McAdams make her a victim anymore."

Sabrina gave him a wicked, private smile. "So I have you to myself."

"All night." His mouth found hers, and he kissed her softly, and when he pulled back, she was nearly breathless.

"Rosie's going to love you," he said. "She's talked to me about how much she admires you—your work ethic, the way you don't give up on anyone, your sense of responsibility. And she knows... I was going through a really—" he gave a short, mirthless laugh "—really dark time. And when I was with you, you gave me some peace." He let her go, took her hands in his, and they stood in the quiet of the late morning, at the edge of the forest that she loved again. "I know we have a lot of baggage, and that might be hard to handle sometimes. We don't have to talk about marriage right now—you and Rosie should get to know each other. But I wanted you to know that that's my ultimate goal. Which my daughter has given her blessing to."

She laughed, tears in her eyes. "I think she's hoping I'll distract you so you'll stop worrying about her so much."

He squeezed her hands, then lifted one of his to her face, smoothing his fingers along a loose tendril of her hair. "I want to see if you could love us as much as I love you."

Sabrina covered his hand with hers, turning her head to press her lips against his palm. "Too late," she said. "I already do."

* * * * *

*Set in darkness beyond the ordinary
world. Passionate tales of life and death.
With characters' lives ruled by laws the
everyday world can't begin to imagine.*

n●cturne

*It's time to discover the
Raintree trilogy…*

New York Times bestselling author
LINDA HOWARD
brings you the dramatic first book
RAINTREE: INFERNO

*The Ansara Wizards are rising and the
Raintree clan must rejoin the battle
against their foes, testing their powers,
relationships and forcing upon them lives
they never could have imagined before…*

*Turn the page for a sneak preview
of the captivating first book
in the Raintree trilogy,*
RAINTREE: INFERNO
by LINDA HOWARD
On sale April 25.

Dante Raintree stood with his arms crossed as he watched the woman on the monitor. The image was in black and white to better show details; color distracted the brain. He focused on her hands, watching every move she made, but what struck him most was how uncommonly *still* she was. She didn't fidget or play with her chips, or look around at the other players. She peeked once at her down card, then didn't touch it again, signaling for another hit by tapping a fingernail on the table. Just because she didn't seem to be paying attention to the other players, though, didn't mean she was as unaware as she seemed.

"What's her name?" Dante asked.

"Lorna Clay," replied his chief of security, Al Rayburn.

"At first I thought she was counting, but she doesn't pay enough attention."

"She's paying attention, all right," Dante murmured. "You just don't see her doing it." A card counter had to remember every card played. Supposedly counting cards was impossible with the number of decks used by the casinos, but there were those rare individuals who could calculate the odds even with multiple decks.

"I thought that, too," said Al. "But look at this piece of tape coming up. Someone she knows comes up to her and speaks, she looks around and starts chatting, completely misses the play of the people to her left—and doesn't look around even when the deal comes back to her, just taps that finger. And damn if she didn't win. Again."

Dante watched the tape, rewound it, watched it again. Then he watched it a third time. There had to be something he was missing, because he couldn't pick out a single giveaway.

"If she's cheating," Al said with something like respect, "she's the best I've ever seen."

"What does your gut say?"

Al scratched the side of his jaw, considering. Finally, he said, "If she isn't cheating, she's the luckiest person walking. She wins. Week in, week out, she wins. Never a huge amount, but I ran the numbers and she's into us for about five grand a week. Hell, boss, on her way out of the casino she'll stop by a slot machine, feed a dollar in and walk away with at least fifty. It's never the same machine, either. I've had her watched, I've had her followed, I've even looked for the same faces in the casino every time she's in here, and I can't find a common denominator."

"Is she here now?"

"She came in about half an hour ago. She's playing blackjack, as usual."

"Bring her to my office," Dante said, making a swift decision. "Don't make a scene."

"Got it," said Al, turning on his heel and leaving the security center.

Dante left, too, going up to his office. His face was calm. Normally he would leave it to Al to deal with a cheater, but he was curious. How was she doing it? There were a lot of bad cheaters, a few good ones, and every so often one would come along who was the stuff of which legends were made: the cheater who didn't get caught, even when people were alert and the camera was on him—or, in this case, her.

It was possible to simply be lucky, as most people understood luck. Chance could turn a habitual loser into a big-time winner. Casinos, in fact, thrived on that hope. But luck itself wasn't habitual, and he knew that what passed for luck was often something else: cheating. And there was the other kind of luck, the kind he himself possessed, but it depended not on chance but on who and what he was. He knew it was an innate power and not Dame Fortune's erratic smile. Since power like his was rare, the odds made it likely the woman he'd been watching was merely a very clever cheat.

Her skill could provide her with a very good living, he thought, doing some swift calculations in his head. Five grand a week equaled $260,000 a year, and that was just from his casino. She probably hit them all, careful to keep the numbers relatively low so she stayed under the radar.

He wondered how long she'd been taking him, how long she'd been winning a little here, a little there, before Al noticed.

The curtains were open on the wall-to-wall window in his office, giving the impression, when one first opened the door, of stepping out onto a covered balcony. The glazed window faced west, so he could catch the sunsets. The sun was low now, the sky painted in purple and gold. At his home in the mountains, most of the windows faced east, affording him views of the sunrise. Something in him needed both the greeting and the goodbye of the sun. He'd always been drawn to sunlight, maybe because fire was his element to call, to control.

He checked his internal time: four minutes until sundown. Without checking the sunrise tables every day, he knew exactly when the sun would slide behind the mountains. He didn't own an alarm clock. He didn't need one. He was so acutely attuned to the sun's position that he had only to check within himself to know the time. As for waking at a particular time, he was one of those people who could tell himself to wake at a certain time, and he did. That talent had nothing to do with being Raintree, so he didn't have to hide it; a lot of perfectly ordinary people had the same ability.

He had other talents and abilities, however, that did require careful shielding. The long days of summer instilled in him an almost sexual high, when he could feel contained power buzzing just beneath his skin. He had to be doubly careful not to cause candles to leap into flame just by his presence, or to start wildfires with a glance in the dry-as-tinder brush. He loved Reno; he didn't want to burn it down. He just felt so damn *alive* with all the sunshine pouring down that he wanted to let the energy pour through him instead of holding it inside.

This must be how his brother Gideon felt while pulling lightning, all that hot power searing through his muscles, his veins. They had this in common, the connection with raw power. All the members of the far-flung Raintree clan had some power, some heightened ability, but only members of the royal family could channel and control the earth's natural energies.

Dante wasn't just of the royal family, he was the Dranir, the leader of the entire clan. "Dranir" was synonymous with king, but the position he held wasn't ceremonial, it was one of sheer power. He was the oldest son of the previous Dranir, but he would have been passed over for the position if he hadn't also inherited the power to hold it.

Behind him came Al's distinctive knock on the door. The outer office was empty, Dante's secretary having gone home hours before. "Come in," he called, not turning from his view of the sunset.

The door opened, and Al said, "Mr. Raintree, this is Lorna Clay."

Dante turned and looked at the woman, all his senses on alert. The first thing he noticed was the vibrant color of her hair, a rich, dark red that encompassed a multitude of shades from copper to burgundy. The warm amber light danced along the iridescent strands, and he felt a hard tug of sheer lust in his gut. Looking at her hair was almost like looking at fire, and he had the same reaction.

The second thing he noticed was that she was spitting mad.

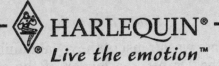

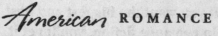
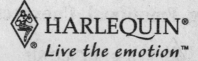

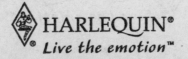

Harlequin® Historical
Historical Romantic Adventure!

Imagine a time of chivalrous knights and unconventional ladies, roguish rakes and impetuous heiresses, rugged cowboys and spirited frontierswomen—these rich and vivid tales will capture your imagination!

Harlequin Historical... they're too good to miss!